HERE'S MUD IN YOUR EYE. . . .

"Mr. Brett," the detective said, "I'll probably be wanting to talk to you in the morning."

"I'll be here," I said, "I hope." They left, and I turned to Marie.

"Another drink, or do you have to go, too?"

She smiled. "This is my night off." My eyebrows went up, and I wondered if I got her implication correctly. Her eyebrows went up, and I gathered I did.

We had another drink or two and managed to stay off the subject of murder. We stayed on the subject of Marie, and I must say I learned quite a bit about her that night. Marie was a remarkable girl. Eventually the gin ran out, so we were forced to retire.

Neither of us got murdered that night. Better things happened. . . .

Bantam Books offers the finest in classic and modern American murder mysteries. Ask your bookseller for the books you have missed.

Rex Stout
Broken Vase
Death of a Dude
Death Times Three
Fer-de-Lance
The Final Deduction
Gambit
The Rubber Band
Too Many Cooks
The Black Mountain
Plot It Yourself
Three for the Chair

Max Allan Collins
The Dark City
Bullet Proof

A. E. Maxwell
Just Another Day in Paradise
Gatsby's Vineyard
The Frog and the Scorpion

Joseph Louis
Madelaine
The Trouble with Stephanie
coming soon: Desert Heat

Mary Jo Adamson
Not Till a Hot January
A February Face
Remember March
April When They Woo
May's Newfangled Mirth

P. M. Carlson
Murder Unrenovated
Rehearsal for Murder

Dick Lupoff
The Comic Book Killer

Margaret Maron
The Right Jack
Baby Doll Games
One Coffee With
Corpus Christmas

Randy Russell
Hot Wire

Marilyn Wallace
Primary Target

William Murray
When The Fat Man Sings
coming soon: The King of the
Madcap

Robert Goldsborough
Murder in E Minor
Death on Deadline
The Bloodied Ivy
coming soon: The Last
Coincidence

Sue Grafton
"A" Is for Alibi
"B" Is for Burglar
"C" Is for Corpse
"D" Is for Deadbeat
"E" Is for Evidence

Joseph Telushkin
The Unorthodox Murder of Rabbi
Wahl
The Final Analysis of Doctor Stark

Richard Hilary
Snake in the Grasses
Pieces of Cream
Pillow of the Community
Behind the Fact

Carolyn G. Hart
Design for Murder
Death on Demand
Something Wicked
Honeymoon With Murder
coming soon: A Little Class on
Murder

Lia Matera
Where Lawyers Fear to Tread
A Radical Departure
The Smart Money
Hidden Agenda

Robert Crais
The Monkey's Raincoat

Keith Peterson
The Trapdoor
There Fell a Shadow
The Rain
coming soon: The Scarred Man

David Handler
The Man Who Died Laughing
The Man Who Lived by Night

WHO'D HIRE BRETT?

John Brett

BANTAM BOOKS
NEW YORK · TORONTO · LONDON · SYDNEY · AUCKLAND

WHO'D HIRE BRETT?
A Bantam Book / published by arrangement with St. Martin's Press

PRINTING HISTORY
St. Martin's Press edition published 1980
Bantam edition / July 1989

ISBN 0-553-27714-6

Published simultaneously in the United States and Canada

Bantam Books are published by Bantam Books, a division of Bantam Double-
day Dell Publishing Group, Inc. Its trademark, consisting of the words
"Bantam Books" and the portrayal of a rooster, is Registered in U.S. Patent
and Trademark Office and in other countries. Marca Registrada. Bantam
Books, 666 Fifth Avenue, New York, New York 10103.

For Mother Becker—
Who tries to keep me out of trouble

I

I never had any intentions of sitting down and taking pen, as it were, in hand. I don't ordinarily do such things, except in cases of extreme emergency. Perhaps a quick note to explain why a bill has failed to show up paid, or a brief jotting explaining that if I should drop out of sight for six months or so, the powers that be need not take undue concern over the situation. (After all, if John Brett chooses to disappear for six months, that's really nobody's concern but John Brett's, is it?) At any rate, I happened to mention to my friend Carl one day that I had a story to tell, and he said why don't you write it down, and I said that I just might do that, and he said you ought to get started, and I said I'd do that one of these first days, and he said you ought to get to it, and I suppose, if truth be known (as it very seldom is), that I really ought to. Next time I have a tale to tell I should simply pretend I know nothing. That's what most people assume I know anyway.

Now, I generally tend to mind my own business. Not, of course, that there's all that much business to tend anymore, since I've left my native soil and come to Los Angeles. Or, at least, thought I left my native soil. As it turned out, what I had thought was my native soil wasn't actually my native soil, but my adopted soil, if such a thing is possible. It doesn't make any difference, really, in the final analysis, though, because the adoption took place at an early enough age that the adopted soil might just as well have been native, if you follow me.

At any rate, the native (or adopted, as the case may be) soil was English, and in the process of tending my business there I fear I may have overtended just a bit. It seems I got involved in something of a scandal at rather high levels. Not in government, of course, but in that rather overextended family that used to run Europe as something of a private garden party, complete with occasional war games and first dibs on all the money that happened to be floating around. Now, of course, the family doesn't run the show, but the people keep them around on a sort of annual retainer, complete with clothes and lodging, and trot them out for formal occasions when a little show is necessary but the people in government have better things to do. The family is expected to keep its collective nose fairly clean, which just about stretches its capabilities to the limit, and I'm afraid that I, in the course of tending to business, discovered a rather dirty handkerchief. Well, to make a long story short, it's a lot easier to replace one John Brett than an entire national institution, so I left England with something of a cloud over my head. Which, when you stop to consider the weather there, isn't hard to do.

So I came to Los Angeles and set up business here, which doesn't really amount to much besides depositing the hush-money checks in the local Charter Bank of London. (One must keep up some of the old ties, and, besides, I find CBL much friendlier than Barclays.)

I've set up light housekeeping in a building called the French Château, which is neither French, nor, properly speaking, a château, being, rather, an apartment house that was built in the thirties by a long-forgotten and probably dead cinema star. It isn't exactly what I might have chosen given the income I might have wanted, but then, considering the state of the British economy, hush money isn't what it might be, either. However, all things set equal, it suffices, and I generally sit quietly in my rooms, watching life (what there is of it) go by on West Ninth Street. (A rather unimaginative name, that; I should think, with the Spanish background here, they might at least have called it *Calle El Nuevo*. Perhaps I shall start a campaign to that effect.)

I tend to live quietly, stirring forth now and then to occasional art openings and theatrical affairs, and, by dint of bandying about my continental background, am on rather cozy terms with what passes as the local aristocracy. My friend Carl tells me that the real aristocracy all live in the East and don't waste much time on the local crop, but I never get East, and the locals seem to put up a fairly good show of it. They don't put much stock in family background, of course, but then I don't have much family background anyway—it has yet to be determined where the Bretts were during the Wars of the Roses; perhaps tending another garden altogether. So I live quietly and stay out of trouble. Most of the time.

II

I'd been pottering about, sweeping up the sweepings from the latest in what appears to be an endless series of local earthquakes, and hoping the landlord would soon appear with his little trowel to stoke up the more major ruptures in the walls, when the phone rang. This, of course, is not a terribly unusual thing for a telephone to do, but under the circumstances, it being shortly after four in the morning (earthquakes, like death, come at strange hours), the jangling gave me pause. Then, assuming it to be some friend or other calling to see if I survived the jolt and to tell me to "wait for the Big One," I answered it. A tactical error.

No friend was at the other end, I can assure you. Rather, it was a somewhat hysterical female voice, at a volume that caused a few more loose pieces of paint to settle on the freshly swept parquet.

"John," she bellowed, "is that you?"

Now, just who she imagined it would be is quite beyond me, but, since she seemed to assume that I would have the place full of strangers, I decided to play along.

5

"No," I said, assuming just the trace of a Ukrainian accent. "This is Tsar Nicholas. Is the revolution over? May I go home now?" It gave her pause.

"John," she repeated, the hysteria lessening only slightly, "please don't try to be funny. My icon is missing."

That, at least, identified my caller. Now, most of the people I know have one or another items about the house that could be classified as *objets d'art*, but only one of them would refer to such a thing as an icon. That was Edith Wilson. Before I go on, I suppose I should tell you a little about Edith.

She goes by Edie, which says something right there. She is married to Harry Wilson, who is generally unidentifiable except by dollar signs and buildings with his name on them. Harry is pleasant enough, if one is sufficiently aware of him to find out. About all that can be said of him is that he makes money and stays in the background. Edie spends money and stays in the foreground. I suppose the easiest way to distinguish the two of them from one another is by driving out Wilshire Boulevard. There are a lot of Wilson buildings. The private ones that show a profit are Harry's. The public ones that don't are Edie's. She runs an establishment called The Bullseye, where you can get a dose of bad steak and bad art for the price of a good Broadway show, but since New York is a long way off, we're more or less stuck with Edie Wilson. At the moment, for me it was more more than less. So it was back to the icon.

"Oh, really?" I said, thinking that four in the morning was a rather intriguing time to be reporting such a thing to the likes of me. "Who do you suppose napped it?"

"I know perfectly well who 'napped' it, as you put it," she said, the hysteria giving way to something of a snarl. "What I want is for you to get it back for me."

I felt it was time to call a halt to the whole proceedings.

"Now, really, Edie, it's four-fifteen in the morning, there's just been an earthquake, which is the only reason I'm functioning at all, and I have a thousand things to do if and when the sun ever comes up." I didn't, but I saw no percentage in letting her think I had a little extra time. Idle hands are Edie's delight. "Besides, if you know who has the bloody thing, why don't you just ring up the police and have them dash around and repossess it?" It seemed logical.

It also seemed to pull her together. The hysteria disappeared, and her voice took on an icy edge I really could have done without. Icy edges are all very well in their place, mind you, but this just didn't seem to be the place, at least not to me. To Edie, apparently, the old icy edge was going to be the thing of the moment.

"John," she said, fairly tingling over the instrument, "are you going to refuse me?"

"Why, the thought hadn't even crossed my mind." It had, of course, but I like to play my hand close to my chest. "But you might elucidate the situation for me a bit. After all, if I'm to turn felon for you, I think I ought to be privy to the details. You know, little things like what the bloody icon looks like, and where it's presently residing, and who has it and other pertinent information. And why now?" Patience was fraying like an old cuff.

"I know it seems odd," she began. It did. Distinctly odd. But then, *much* of America seems odd. "But it isn't really odd when you think about it." Not that I had had, ten minutes earlier, any particular intention of thinking about it, but times change. I was listening, and I was thinking, and I should have stuck to my sweeping.

"It's that little black Mud Dancer."

I cast about in my mind but was unable to identify this Mud Dancer, little, black or otherwise, among our mutual acquaintances. I mentioned the fact, but Edie, as usual, had an answer.

"The icon. It's a Guinean Mud Dancer, about six inches high. That man Gotham, who lives above you, stole it."

Now, this Gotham is a quiet, inoffensive sort of little man, a decorator, if memory served, who didn't seem at all the type to be napping Edith Wilson's Mud Dancer. Further probing was obviously called for.

"Are you sure?"

"Oh, John, of course I'm sure. Here's what happened."

At last, I thought, sleep is just around the corner. As it turned out, something else entirely was just around the bloody corner.

Edith continued: "Gotham was here this afternoon, or yesterday afternoon, rather, looking over Harry's den. He saw the icon and wanted to know where I got it. Well, as it happens, it's not in the country exactly legally at the moment. A customs mix-up, or something. Anyway, I didn't tell him much, and he dropped the whole thing. But after he left, *right* after he left, the icon was gone. I talked to Harry, but he didn't want me to call the police; he was afraid they'd impound it because of the lack of papers. We've been trying to figure out what to do ever since, and then I remembered you live almost underneath Gotham, and with the earthquake I figured you'd be awake, and . . . are you following me?"

"Unfortunately, yes. I suppose you want me to dash right up there this minute, latch onto the thing and trot it over to you?" I'm afraid a note of hysteria had begun to creep into my own voice at that point. "My God, Edie, where would I even look for it? And what if I get caught?"

"He's not there. I just phoned, and no one answered. As for where it is, he has a collection of Mud Dancers in a cabinet in the living room. I'm sure that's where mine is. You can recognize it because one toe is gone."

"How convenient." I'm afraid my note of sarcasm was lost on her. Edie isn't much of a one for notes of sarcasm.

"Well, will you do it?"

Ordinarily, I would have issued flat-out regrets on the invitation, but in this particular case there were other considerations. Edie had done me quite a few favors and, in spite of her predilection for odd art, was really a good sort, and it wasn't as if Gotham's place was half a continent away, and life had been rather quiet, and the sense of adventure reared its

ugly head and, well . . . you know how these things
go. In short, she suckered me in.

"Oh, all right. But what do you want me to do
with it once I have it?"

"I'll have Harry leave right now and meet you at
the corner of Wilshire and Hobart. It should take
him between thirty and forty minutes from here. Is
that enough time?"

"If it isn't, it will be because I've had a heart attack and will be found dead on the premises at
dawn, the Mud Dancer clutched, lilylike, to my
breast."

She chuckled, which I hadn't really expected.

"Good. And John, thanks so much. You don't
know what this means to me." She clicked off.

Well, I thought, I might just as well get to it. Actually, I didn't really expect any trouble. I have quite a
few extra keys littering up the place, and I figured if
my own key didn't fit the Gotham manse one of the
others probably would. I didn't worry about the
niceties, such as surgical gloves, partly because I
didn't have any and partly because I didn't see what
Gotham could do even if he found out about the
theft. I mean, when you've swiped an item that
wasn't legally where you swiped it from, and then
someone else swipes it from you, you aren't going to
be terribly anxious to sound the alarm, are you? So
off I went.

It went remarkably well, all things considered.
My key didn't, indeed, slip Gotham's old bolt, but
the third one I tried did, and I simply slid in. There
was the cabinet, complete with Mud Dancers, and
there was Edie's, with the incriminating broken toe.

I opened the cabinet, picked it up, closed the cabinet and off I went, slick as you please, me and my Mud Dancer.

Within the allotted thirty to forty minutes, there I stood, at the corner of Wilshire and Hobart, wrapped in an old trench coat I keep around for such occasions, with the icon wrapped in what I thought was a remarkably brown paper bag. And then, right on schedule, old Harry turned up. He pulled over to the curb, rolled down the window and stuck his quiet unassuming head out.

"Sorry to drag you out like this, John, but you know how Edie is."

"Nothing to it, Harry. Always glad to be of help." For a second, I thought there should have been a code word or something, but then, I'm not likely to misidentify old Harry, am I? So I slipped him the icon, and off he went. Well, that's that, I thought.

As I watched him drive off, I thought, considering it's quarter of five in the morning, and a theft has just been committed, and a secret rendezvous, and all that, wouldn't it be interesting if a big black sedan, maybe a Buick or a Cadillac, or even a Rolls, were to pull up and someone were to pump old Harry full of holes?

Which is precisely what happened, at precisely that moment.

III

Well, it was unexpected, I'll say that for it. I mean, there I was, just as calm as toast in my trench coat, and then, well, bang, bang, bang. Just like in the movies, if you know what I mean. So then, of course, the question became one of what, as it were, the shrewd thing for John Brett to do was.

Well, I don't know what someone else might have done, but as for me, what's done is done, and I scooted right on back home, a matter of three short blocks. And, if I may say so, those three short blocks lengthened perceptibly in the time it took me to scoot them. After all, one never knows when the old black sedan might come for one, does one?

Safe back in my rooms, I considered what to do. The thought of calling the police occurred, I will admit, but then I remembered the Mud Dancer, with the personal fingerprints no doubt prominently displayed. The fuzz, in a word, was out. Edie was in.

I dialed her. On the second ring, blessedly, the instrument was answered: "This is Edie Wilson . . ."

"Edie, is that you?"

". . . Currently I am not at home. If you . . ."

"Oh, for God's sake!"

". . . will leave a message . . ."

It was one of those damned answering things. A sudden vision of my leaving a message that Harry had just been gunned down on Wilshire Boulevard crossed my mind. Instinct told me to hang up. I sputtered something incoherent, as I do now and then in situations such as this, when I was saved.

"John, I'm terribly sorry," Edie's voice came over in a sort of overlay of the blasted recording. "John, are you still there?"

I gasped. "Yes. Yes, I'm still here. What on earth was that all about?"

"I was fixing myself a drink. I always leave the thing on, so if I don't want to talk to whoever calls, I can still get the message. Is everything all right?"

I wondered how to break it to her, then decided that a straight shot at it was probably best.

"I'm afraid not. Harry got shot." There was a long silence, and I thought perhaps I should have done better to have gone over to see the old girl.

"John," she said at last, "I thought you said Harry got shot."

"I'm sorry, Edie, but I'm afraid that's what I did say."

"Oh, my God." I hoped she had the drink handy.

"It all seemed to go so well. I gave him the icon, and he pulled away, and well, someone pulled up and shot him."

I could hear her crying, but it was all I could say. Well, after all, what *can* you say?

"But . . . but . . . who . . . ?"

"Well . . ." What I had to tell her now was particularly difficult. Nonetheless, one must say what
one must say.

"Edie, I'm afraid it was your car."

"What?"

"The car the person was in. It was yours."

"But that's ridiculous."

"It was a black Bentley, and it had your plate on it.
That new one. E D I E. A rather stupid idea of the
governor's, if you ask me."

"But my car is in the garage here. I know it is."

"Well, maybe it was, but it isn't now." For some
reason, don't ask me what, I thought she needed
me. "Shall I come over?"

"Will you, John? I don't think I can go through
this by myself. Did you call the police?"

"No . . ."

"You didn't? Why not?"

"Well . . . the Mud Dancer, you know . . ."

"Oh. But . . . well, they'll have to be called. Oh,
John, what am I to do?"

Her? Well, I didn't like that very much, I can tell
you. After all, it was my prints on that damned icon,
not hers, and I'll grant you that the loss of a husband
is no laughing matter, but a simple burglary seemed
to me to be fast turning into what I think they call a
"murder one." Then it occurred to me that if I vol-
unteered to call the police myself, I could sort of
swing by the scene of the crime, as it were, scoop up
the bloody icon and *then* call the police. By the time
they arrived, I should be far away, icon once again in
hand. Better to be caught with a hot icon than a dead
body.

"Don't worry about it, Edie. I'll take care of everything and be right there."

I didn't even wait for her to say good-bye. I grabbed my coat and was on my way. Of course, I had to face the ugly possibility that by the time I got back up to Wilshire, the police might very well have discovered the grisly mess. I chose to ignore that particular ugly possibility.

It was a dead heat. Just as I pulled up to Harry's car from the east, a patrol car pulled up from the west. We met at Harry's. The car had slowed up on the sidewalk and was resting comfortably against the front of a bank. Harry was resting comfortably against the steering wheel. The icon was gone.

I thought as quickly and as clearly as I could under the circumstances, and I will be the first to admit that speed and clarity were not what they might have been. However, it did seem to me that I might have something of a time trying to explain that I had seen the murder, run three blocks back home to get my car, then come back to the scene of the crime without ever having taken time out to call the police. It seemed to me that perhaps an anonymous tip at some future date might be more convenient for my social calendar than trying to explain at the moment how I happened to know the license of the other car.

Thus went the mental processes. I made all the proper tut-tuttings one makes when on the premises with the newly dead, expressed my hopes for an early solution to the police and took my leave.

By the time I got to Beverly Hills, Edie seemed to have gone into a state of shock. She sat quite still in her study, her fist wrapped around a drink, her coat over her shoulders. I didn't say anything at first but mixed myself a drink. After the preceding events, I figured I needed one. Then I turned to her.

"Well, the police know what's happened."

"Did you call them?"

"No, I didn't have to. I figured I might just as well pick up the Mud Dancer before calling. As it turned out, that was unnecessary. A patrol car got there just as I did. But the icon was already gone."

"Gone?"

"Yes. Whoever shot Harry must have picked it up right afterward."

"Poor Harry. What shall I do now?"

"Oh, you'll be all right."

"No, I don't think I will. Harry was more to me than anybody thought. Oh, he was quiet, and I wasn't, but sometimes I was. And when I was quiet, I needed him very much. And he was always there."

Well, you can't say much to a speech like that, so I didn't try. Instead, I sort of tweaked at her coat.

"Going somewhere?"

"What?" Then she seemed to come out of it a little. "Oh. No. I just went out to check my car. It's there, but the motor's warm. John, who would steal my car and kill my husband?"

She seemed quite helpless. I touched her hand.

"Someone, I should say, who wanted to have you blamed for it."

"But that's so ridiculous!"

"It would seem so, wouldn't it?"

It was then that the police arrived. I've noticed that in America the police seem to feel that there's some sort of perverted virtue in reporting a disaster at the earliest possible moment. As if there would be something immoral in letting someone have a spot of breakfast before ruining their day. At any rate, what with the wonders of modern technology, the Beverly Hills P. D. seemed already well apprised of the situation. One Sergeant Steinberg appeared, ushered in by the maid, who had apparently roused herself at some point during the proceedings. I took the opportunity to order breakfast, since it appeared that the rest of the day was probably pretty well shot.

"Mrs. Wilson?" inquired this Steinberg.

"Yes. Sit down. I already know what you're going to tell me." Steinberg looked a little surprised, and I must say, it sent a bit of a shock through me. Things began to look a bit sticky.

"About your husband?"

Edie nodded. "John told me. Oh, I didn't make the introductions. This is John Brett, a friend of my husband's and mine."

The sergeant's gaze shifted to me, and the room somehow seemed suddenly warm. Downright stifling, if truth be known.

"And how did you know what happened, Mr. Brett?"

"Ah . . . well, I . . . um . . . yes . . . well, what happened was this." The temperature in the room rose another hundred degrees or so. "Well, it's a rather remarkable coincidence, but I saw it happen." Steinberg looked fairly astounded, and I can't really say I blamed him.

"Would you mind telling me about it?"

Well, I thought, it's going to be a mite sticky, but I'll give it a whirl. I cleared my throat (or gasped for air, depending on how you look at it). Then I made a clean breast of it and told all. Somehow, it sounded a bit unlikely, but there was Harry, dead, and there was me, in the midst of it all. Steinberg didn't seem overly impressed.

"Mr. Brett, do you expect me to believe all that?" I hoped I didn't look as silly as I felt. Steinberg turned to Edie. "Mrs. Wilson?"

"It's exactly as he told you, Sergeant. I know it doesn't sound plausible, but, well . . ." She began to cry. "Oh, John, I'm so sorry to have gotten you involved in all this. Harry was so sure it would work out all right."

"Harry? Your husband?"

Edie looked up. "Well, of course. It was Harry's plan. He didn't want the theft of the Mud Dancer reported to the police."

Steinberg frowned. "This Mud Dancer. Exactly what was it?"

Edie thought a moment. "It's a clay figurine of a Guinean Mud Dancer. It's sort of dark gray, almost black, about six inches tall, with one toe broken off."

"Do you know why your husband didn't want to report its theft?"

"He said something about its not being in the country legally."

"What did he mean by that?"

"I suppose it's like quite a few of our things. Do you know anything about National Treasure Acts?"

"National Treasure Acts?"

"Yes. Quite a few countries have them now. I think they started with Egypt. They're laws prohibiting the removal from a country of any art objects or historical items found in that country. Well, Harry and I are collectors, and collectors, um, don't always observe the National Treasure Acts. Or, at least, we don't always make sure our agents are observing them. That's why some of our things are never shown publicly or auctioned. The countries of origin could impound them and prosecute the owners. I think there's some kind of international agreement."

"And this Mud Dancer fell under such an act?"

"I don't know. Harry didn't actually say, and I didn't ask him."

Steinberg nodded. "Well, Mr. Brett, I think you're off lucky this time. We'll have to talk to this Gotham fellow, but I don't imagine he'll want to prosecute. After all, he'd have to admit to having stolen goods in order to do it, wouldn't he? He probably won't even admit he ever had the Mud Dancer. As for the murder, well, don't either one of you leave town."

That made both of us jump a bit, I can tell you.

"Well, look at it from my point of view. Each of you backs up the other one's story. The Mud Dancer is missing, and it's really the crucial point of the whole thing. For all I know, you could have plotted it all between the two of you." Well, that just about tore it for Edie.

"Sergeant Steinberg, that's the most disgusting thing I've ever heard. Please leave my house!"

Steinberg's eyebrows rose just a hair. "Before you call the police?" he asked, with just a hint of a sneer in his voice. Well, I'm no more for hints of sneers than Edie is for notes of sarcasm, but I decided to let it pass. The soup seemed plenty thick enough already. Edie wasn't so easily cowed.

"No, I won't call the police. I'll call my lawyer. Now, either arrest us both, or leave."

Steinberg seemed to consider, which did no good for the state of my nerves. I've never seen the interior of an American jail, and the idea of an enforced tour simply didn't appeal. Finally, he stood up. For my part, I don't think I could have.

"Very well, Mrs. Wilson. However, I should tell you this. As soon as I leave, I'll get a search warrant. In the meantime, I'll ask you not to leave your house. I don't really expect to find anything, but I intend to have a look." And that was the end of the first interview with Steinberg.

The maid came in immediately afterward with breakfast. Edie was still snarling. The maid looked worn.

"Is he gone, Marie?"

"Yes, ma'am."

"Marie, you may want to be leaving yourself."

"Ma'am?"

"Mr. Wilson has been murdered, and the police seem to think that Mr. Brett and I did it."

"Oh, ma'am!"

"Yes. 'Oh, ma'am.' At any rate, if you want to leave, I'll understand."

"Yes, ma'am. I'll let you know, ma'am." She disappeared.

"Well," sighed Edie, "I don't know what to do. John, I'm terribly sorry. I wish I'd never called you tonight."

What could I say? I wished she hadn't, too. The comforting pat seemed called for, so I administered it.

"I suppose I'd better start arranging for the funeral." Her eyes widened. "They will let me have one, won't they? Or will they have to hold the . . . the remains?"

"Oh, I shouldn't think so. I don't see why they'd need an autopsy. After all, there isn't much question of how he died. Only who did it. And they seem to have pretty well decided that issue, too, don't they?"

"Yes." Edie slumped on the sofa for a moment, then straightened up. "Yes, they have. So I guess it's up to us to set them straight. John, we'd better find that Mud Dancer."

My stomach sank back into my shoes. I'd more or less come to grips with the possibility of being tried. But going on a search for the evidence really didn't do a thing for me. Not a thing.

IV

By eight o'clock that morning—which is a poor hour on the best of mornings, and this was hardly the best of mornings—I was busily engaged in uncharitable thoughts about a policeman named Steinberg. I mean, really. The man had suggested that I, me, John Brett, might be the hypotenuse in what could only be described as a very tired triangle. Now, I am not considered by my friends (which were legion at last count) to be unattractive. Nor have I ever lacked for company of what is delicately called the gentler sex. (It has been my experience that the majority of that sex are neither delicate nor gentle, but one makes allowances for convention.) Needless to say, it didn't please me to be accused by the local constabulary of being involved in what the English call a bloody mess with Edie and the late H. Wilson. Not, of course, that the late H. was necessarily involved, except in the rather minor role of odd man out, but still, the whole thing reeked of things that my ancestors would definitely not have discussed in polite company.

I guess what it boiled down to was this. I am still on the sunny side of thirty. Edie, on the other hand, is . . . well, let me put it this way. Edie's been counting backwards for five years, and she just hit forty-five. And here was this Steinberg insinuating a . . . well, insinuating a *liaison* between us. Most upsetting. Most upsetting, indeed.

So there I was, mulling over the possibility of becoming persona non grata in the locality, when Marie appeared, coffeepot in hand. I'd seen her before of course, but always in the midst of a crowd, and always behind a cocktail tray or a plate of caviar. Now I more or less sized her up. The first thing I noticed was that there was a lot of size there.

Marie was a tall girl, probably close to five feet ten, and she looked decidedly unservantlike. Not a trace of cloying servility to her whatsoever, if you know what I mean. She definitely wouldn't have fitted into any of the better English homes: most of the guests would have mistaken her for visiting royalty and tossed their hats and coats to the hostess without so much as a "good evening." She was that type of girl. Stately, that's what she was. And damned attractive, too. Red hair, which I've always been partial to, and a sort of heart-shaped face. Not icky Melanie Wilkes heart-shaped, but the hair definitely formed a peak on the forehead. Sort of Mary Queen of Scots heart-shaped.

She sailed in with the fresh supply of coffee and set it down. Then she just stood there, looking at Edie.

"Ma'am?"

Edie looked up. "Oh, Marie. Have you made up your mind?"

"Yes, ma'am. I've decided to stay."

Edie looked a bit surprised. "Are you sure? It might not be the wisest thing for you to do."

"May I sit down a moment, ma'am?" Now Edie looked definitely surprised, but she indicated a chair. Marie sat, and the "ma'am" attitude in her disappeared altogether.

"Mrs. Wilson, I've enjoyed working here. I like you, and I liked Mr. Wilson, and I don't think you or Mr. Brett had anything to do with killing him. Of course, I don't really have anything to back up that feeling except instinct, but I've followed my instincts before, and usually they aren't wrong. If they are this time, they are. Granted, no one will want a maid who was in a house where there was a scandal like this could turn out to be, but then, I don't intend to be a maid much longer, anyway. If you don't mind, I'll stay around."

Well, that set Edie back a bit. I mean, maids don't ordinarily just stop being maids at will, as it were. I wondered what she was planning, and since women don't usually pry into the personal lives of the hired help, I decided that snoopy friends like me might just as well.

"Getting married?" I said, giving her the bright smile.

"No, nothing like that. I'm going to become an art dealer."

"But you don't know anything about that," Edie protested.

"Oh, I know a little more than you might think. My father was a dealer until he died. And my uncle is still one."

"Keller? I've never heard of a dealer named Keller."

Marie smiled. "It's my uncle on my mother's side. James Hinman."

Well, the name didn't impress me, but then I don't run too much with the artsy set. Lay on me the name of any good polo player and I'll perk right up, but art dealers, well, no. It certainly seemed to light a fire under Edie, though. I thought she was going to drop her cup.

"James Hinman! *The* James Hinman?"

Marie began laughing, and the sound certainly did a lot to relieve the strain that had been building in that room all morning. It was a sound like oil on the proverbial waters. Soothing, that's what it was.

Well, at any rate, I gathered through the above laughter that Marie's uncle was indeed *the* James Hinman and that he was what they call well regarded in old-art circles. It's a circle, as I say, that I've never really aspired to, but I suppose there are those to whom it's important. Certainly, old Edie was impressed.

"But if he's your uncle, why work for me? Why not work for him—as a sort of apprentice, or something?"

"That's next," Marie answered. "We talked it over a long time ago and decided that if I started with him, everyone would think of me as his assistant, and I'd never get anywhere till he died. But if I came in with some knowledge, particularly in a special field, I'd have some respect right from the start. When I heard you people needed a maid, it fit right in. Where better to learn about primitive art than here? Most of the best stuff in the country comes through this house, and all the people I'll eventually need to know have been here at one time or another. I may only have served them a drink or two, but I keep my ears open. When I'm ready, they'll know who I am.

Well, that sounded sinister to me. When I think of all the perfectly good families that have had the whistle blown on them by servants who knew too much, it makes me positively quiver. I must say, though, that it certainly didn't bother Edie.

"Why, John," she said in a tone that usually indicates impending fatuousness, "don't you think that's enterprising of her?"

"Enterprising" wasn't the word I would have put to it. "Devious" seemed much more to the point, but often, I've noticed, Americans see things in an entirely different light from us English. That Revolution thing, for instance. Now, it never occurred to us that the provincials might get upset about a little thing like a tea tax. After all, how could we govern them without having a means of financing the whole thing? But the Americans, as I say, have a different way of looking at things, so I made the proper sounds.

"Oh, very," I said, smiling the bright smile. Then I decided a little probing might be in order. "Just what do you mean, they'll know who you are?"

This Marie turned out to be a sharp girl. She guessed at once, bless her heart, that I suspected she might have a taint of the blackmailer in her blood.

"Nothing bad, Mr. Brett. But perhaps you've noticed that if someone comes up to you and, say, asks after the health of your Aunt Mary, you're not likely to admit you don't recognize them."

Now, I don't have an Aunt Mary, so that ploy wouldn't work with me, but I do remember one occasion when I was passing some time in one of the more disreputable pubs in Soho, when a fellow plopped down beside me and asked if I still had that '53 Jag. Well, I must admit that it wasn't until I'd bought him three pints that I remembered that he'd once stolen the thing from me. I got her point. I also decided it was time for me to leave.

Marie accompanied me to the door, and I sensed that she wanted to ask me something. I fiddled with the trench coat. She fiddled with a button on her blouse. It crossed my mind that I might enjoy fiddling with the buttons on her blouse myself, but my good breeding stood me in good stead.

"Mr. Brett," she began.

"Why don't you call me John?" A dumb thing to say, but there are times when dumb things have to be said. She didn't seem to notice.

"John," she began again, "you don't think she did it, do you?

"Edie? Kill Harry? Of course not. Oh, she's a little weird, but not that weird."

"I hope not. I like her. A lot better than I liked him."

"Harry? He was a nice enough sort." Not that I knew, really, but it seemed like a good thing to stick up for the dead master in front of the servants.

"No he wasn't. He was a cheat."

"That's not a very nice thing to say."

"No, it's not. But it's true. That Mud Dancer, for instance."

"What about it?"

"It's a fake."

"Oh, come now."

"Really, it is. It's not hard to tell. The broken toe."

"What's that got to do with it?"

"The clay underneath was white. If it was real, the clay would be the same color all the way through. The New Guineans aren't too good with paint."

"Well, even if it was a fake, I don't see . . ."

She cut me off. "But John, it's obvious. If that icon was a fake, there couldn't have been a good reason for Mr. Wilson not wanting the theft reported to the police. No one cares about fakes. The National Treasures Acts wouldn't apply."

"Maybe he didn't want anyone to know it was a fake."

"That's not hard. All he would have had to do was say it was a replica. But he didn't. He insisted that the theft of that Mud Dancer couldn't be reported. But it was a worthless fake."

"It doesn't make much sense, does it?"

"No, it doesn't. A lot of things about Harry Wilson didn't make much sense."

I gave her an encouraging look, but she didn't pursue it. After a little more trench-coat fiddling, I left. Just as I was getting into my car, she called to me. I turned back to look at her.

"Mr. Brett," she called, "I forgot to ask you—are you allowed back in London yet?"

I paled. Now, dropping references to someone's Aunt Mary is one thing. Dropping references to the blight on someone's record is entirely another. Obviously, this Marie had a glorious career ahead of her. I suppose my mouth must have been hanging open, because she laughed. I must say, that set everything right again. She disappeared into the house, and I headed for home.

V

Nothing much had changed on the home front. The cracks were still in the walls, the dust was still settling to the floor. I thought about going to bed, but somehow the idea didn't have much going for it. Instead, I brewed a pot of tea and sat down to think things over. I had, I thought, plenty to think about.

I can't really say that the passing of Harry made too much impression on me, one way or the other. I mean, Harry had been Harry, if you follow me, and now he wasn't, and, frankly, who cared? Oh, I supposed there might be a foundation or two that might miss the annual check, but, on the other hand, Edie could probably be counted on to make up the deficit. Idly, I wondered whether or not they'd change Harry's name to black letters on all those buildings, à la Rolls-Royce. Probably not. Sentiment doesn't count for much these days. Not that it had ever been a particularly marketable item, but still . . . my thoughts trailed off. My thoughts often do.

I guess what really bothered me were the allegations with reference to old Harry's integrity. Now, if you'd asked me, Harry was the very soul of integrity (if integrity has a soul, which I, for one, doubt). But then again, you never know. And this Marie seemed a good sort. A trifle unscrupulous, perhaps, but scruples and sentiment seem to have wound up in the same grave. (That probably says something about modern times, but I'm sure I don't know what.)

After much mulling, the processes of which I won't go into here, it occurred to me that it might be a good idea to engage in an interview with the gentleman Gotham. This idea, I realize now, was undoubtedly a function of my lack of sleep. At any rate, it seemed a good idea at the time, and I proceeded to carry it out.

A simple ring of the bell brought the man to the door. He was dressed in a robe and, from all appearances, had just arisen. I thought about apologizing for awakening him, but in view of the fact that I knew damned well he hadn't spent the night at home, I decided to forego it. He looked at me blankly, and I realized he didn't recognize me. Probably didn't spend as much time as I do peering out the old windows.

"Good morning," I fairly chirped, for want of a better opener.

"Yes?"

"I'm John Brett. Live downstairs."

"Yes?"

"I . . . uh . . . I wondered how you came through the quake?"

"I did."

Things didn't seem to be going too well. "I wonder if I might come in?"

"Why?"

Well, now that stopped me. Why, indeed? Certainly, the man was being less than cordial, and he
wasn't exactly my cup of tea anyway. Sixty-five-
year-old men who wear bad wigs and flared pants
may be all right in some places, but they really aren't
for me. Not that I had anything against him; it's just
that he wasn't anyone I would have chosen to spend
a night on the town with. But still and all, I did want
to talk to him. I decided deviousness was the order
of the day.

"Well, actually, when the earthquake hit, I went
outside. No lights came on in your apartment, so I
came up to find out if you were all right. You weren't
home."

"No, I wasn't."

"Well, uh, I noticed your collection . . . and, um,
well . . ."

He perked up quite noticeably. "You came in?"

"Well, yes, actually, I did. The door wasn't
locked." I figured there wasn't any way he could
prove it one way or another, and it might warm
things up a bit.

"Perhaps you'd better come in, Mr. Brett." He
opened the door wider, and I went in. Gotham
wasn't alone. With him in the apartment was a
young man whom I can best describe as being large
and not too friendly looking.

"Sorry. Didn't realize you had company."

"It's all right. Troy, this is Mr. Brett. He was here
last night." Why is it, I wonder, that young men who

keep company with much older men, and don't do anything else, are always named Troy? If it isn't Troy, it's Lance. Very strange. Probably not relevant, but strange. Anyway, this edition of Troy didn't say anything.

"Yes," I said. "Well, anyway, I noticed your collection."

"So you said."

"It's very interesting. I thought perhaps you'd show it to me in the daylight."

"Mr. Brett, what is it you want? I don't know what possessed you to come up here last night, and I doubt that the door was unlocked. So what is it?"

"Well, actually, what fascinated me was the Mud Dancer." I was ready to go to the cabinet and express shock that the thing was gone.

"You mean that one?" He pointed to an object on the coffee table. I looked at it, all set to brush it off. Unfortunately, it couldn't be brushed off. It was the Mud Dancer, broken toe and all. I tried not to gasp, but I probably wasn't too successful. Where trying not to gasp is concerned, I rarely can pull it off.

"Yes, that's the one. Fascinating thing. Guinean, isn't it?"

"Yes. It's a ceremonial object. Used in a fertility dance, or a war dance, I think."

I thought I'd have a closer look at the thing, so I went over and picked it up. I turned it over a couple of times and looked at the toe. White under the surface.

"Beautiful fake," I said.

Gotham's face darkened perceptibly. "What do you mean, fake?"

"Its been painted. The Guinean natives use gray mud when they make these things. See? Here, where the toe is broken. Who sold it to you?"

Gotham took the object, and the Troy character came over to look, too. Gotham turned the thing over, just as I had, and examined the toe. Then he nodded.

"You're right. OK, Troy."

Everything went black.

I don't know how long I was unconscious, but when I woke up I was back in my own apartment. I glanced at the clock, and it said eight-thirty, so I must have spent most of the day sound asleep. Now, I'm not too bright, but I do know that a simple blow on the head won't keep someone out that long. It seemed like an opportune moment to call the police.

Since Steinberg already knew me, he seemed like the one to call. He wasn't in, but I didn't feel like talking to anyone else. I left a message, then came to the quite unremarkable conclusion that a gin and tonic was in order. It isn't my usual drink, but, under the circumstances, I felt a change of pace was called for. I thought a slug of the old juniper might give me the zip that recent events had drained me of. Unfortunately, there wasn't any gin.

Now, I have discovered, somewhat to my dismay, that in America there are strange priorities. If you need a doctor in a hurry, you might just as well call the undertaker directly and save the message units. Doctors are not considered essential services. Liquor stores are. The solution, of course, is obvious. Never come down with anything that a drink won't cure. Armed with the knowledge that relief was as near as my closest telephone, I clutched at the instrument. Gin, I knew, would soon be at hand. I came up with Marie instead.

There's always something a little bit unsettling about grabbing at a phone and having it yell back at you before you've got it properly in hand. It gives one pause. Seldom, however, does it give one enough pause so that whoever has been rude enough to tie up one's phone in an emergency will give up and go away. Besides, reflexes take over, and one generally picks up the handset with an alacrity that gives the other party the repulsive impression that one is just sitting waiting for a call. Any call. At any rate, when it rang, I answered.

"John?"

Why is it in America nobody ever gives you time to identify yourself? I decided not to affirm the accusation.

"John, is that you?"

"May I help you?"

"Is this John Brett?"

Now that was more like it. "Why, yes."

"Thank God. John, this is Marie. Sergeant Steinberg was just here. They've arrested Mrs. Wilson."

"Why?"

"I don't know, but I know they've found the Mud Dancer."

"They couldn't have. I just saw it myself."

"What?"

"Well, not just now. This morning. It was in Gotham's apartment. Then they hit me."

"John, what are you talking about?"

"I decided to have a talk with Gotham. I went up there, and the Mud Dancer was right there on his coffee table. When I pointed out to him that it was a fake, he had his friend hit me."

"I'd better come over."

"Oh, I don't think . . ."

She cut me off. "Don't be silly. I'll be there in thirty minutes."

"But you don't know where I live."

"I have your address right here. It's in Mrs. Wilson's address book."

The girl was turning out to be remarkably clever. Perhaps ever resourceful.

"Very well. Do you drink gin?"

"Love it."

"Good. I'm ordering in about a decade's supply. After today, I expect to need it."

Marie and the gin arrived simultaneously. I'm not sure which I was more cheered to see. Lord knows each had their separate but equal attractions. I managed to stir up a couple of bracers, while Marie more or less openly checked out the premises. She seemed impressed by the king-sized bed.

"Do you have a lot of company in that?"

"No, I thrash about in my sleep a bit." I didn't see that my sex life was any of her business. Not yet, anyway.

We got ourselves settled in the living room, out of temptation's way, and got down to what I think is referred to as brass tackiness. No, that's not right. Tacks! That's it, brass tacks! At any rate, we got down to them.

"You'd better tell me what happened," Marie said, and I thought I noted a gleam of genuine concern in her eyes. Of course, it could have been drugs, but I preferred to think it was concern.

"Well, I told you. I went up to Gotham's den of iniquity and got coshed by a most unattractive friend of his."

"Where?"

"Right here." I indicated a spot on the old pate that seemed like it might have been a good target for a well-placed cosh. Marie felt it.

"There isn't any lump." Her hands moved over the balance of my cranium, and she pronounced me totally lump-free. I couldn't deny it.

"Well, actually, I think they drugged me, or something."

"Did you drink anything up there?"

"No. It wasn't exactly a social occasion." At that point, she reached over with both fists and clapped me on the upper arms. The right one hurt, and I winced.

"Roll up your sleeve."

I did as bid, and there appeared before the already jaundiced eyes a rather ugly black and blue mark.

"They seem to have used a dull needle," Marie observed. "What did you feel when you woke up? And how long were you out?"

"I must have been out for a good ten hours. And when I woke up, my mouth seemed awfully dry."

"Mmm-hmm. Probably sodium pentathol, or something like that. Well, no permanent harm done. The main question is, why?"

"How would I know?"

"You wouldn't. And neither would I. But I think we ought to find out."

It was my personal opinion that trying to find out would only lead to more trouble, and I thought I'd had plenty of that already. I expressed said opinion to Marie. She was unimpressed.

"John, they've already arrested Mrs. Wilson. From what you both said this morning, I wouldn't be surprised if they weren't thinking of picking you up, too."

As if to bear her out, the doorbell rang. The esteemed Sergeant Steinberg appeared.

"May I come in, Mr. Brett?" Well, I couldn't very well see leaving him on the doorstep and giving the neighbors a floor show.

"Do."

"Thank you." It was said in the tones of an executioner thanking the condemned for fastening his own blindfold. The spirit cringed. The body poured another drink.

"Hello, Miss Keller." Marie nodded to him. Good for you, I thought. Don't ask after his health. With any luck at all, it's failing fast.

"Would you like a drink, Sergeant, or am I to be handcuffed and led away?"

"Now, now, Mr. Brett. Nothing like that. I'd love a drink—"

I started to ooze toward the bar.

"—but I'm on duty."

"But you're not going to arrest me?"

"Not now, no. I suppose Miss Keller told you we picked up Edith Wilson?"

"Yes. How did she take it?"

"Not very well. She called her lawyer, and she's already out. Being rich helps, even in Beverly Hills."

"Being rich doesn't help in Beverly Hills, it's a necessity of life," Marie observed.

"Yes, well, be that as it may," Steinberg said, obviously trying to avoid a discussion of the relative merits of money in dear old B.H. "Mr. Brett, are you sure you were being entirely frank this morning?"

"Surely you don't think I made up a ridiculous story like that?"

"Now, I didn't say you made it up. I just want to know if you told us all of it."

"Every grisly detail."

"Would you mind going over it once more?"

I did (mind), but I did (go over it once more). When I finished, Steinberg seemed to think for a while. Silence settled like smog over the room. Finally, the Beverly Hills oracle spoke.

"A couple of questions."

"Fire at will."

"First, why didn't you call the police right away after you saw the shooting?"

"I told you. I wanted to get the Mud Dancer. After all, it had my fingerprints all over it."

"OK. Now, how long did it take Mrs. Wilson to come on the line when you called her?"

"That machine answered on the first ring. She came on about, oh, not more than half a minute later. Probably less. Why?"

"A couple of things. Mrs. Wilson's phone is hooked into two machines. One is the answering device. The other one automatically relays incoming calls to any other number that it's set for. When the connection is made, the answering machine cuts out."

"Then you mean Mrs. Wilson wasn't necessarily at home when John called?" Marie asked, looking puzzled.

"Exactly."

"What about that relaying machine? Was it set for another number?"

"No, but that doesn't mean that it wasn't, early this morning. We're checking it out."

"How?"

"If it was set for another number, and that number wasn't in the toll-free area, the phone company will have a record of the number called. The relayed call would be billed to the Wilson's phone, not yours."

Marie nodded, then looked baffled by the whole thing and shook her head.

"You said there were two things, Sergeant?" I said.

"Yes. We found the Mud Dancer this morning. Your prints aren't on it. The only prints we found belong to Edith Wilson."

VI

I must say that that last bit of news rather set me up on my toes. I mean, if they had found the Mud Dancer, and my prints were not among those present, then I was rather in the clear, as they say in criminal circles. It didn't look so good for Edie, though, what with the house being cluttered up with incriminating telephonic gadgetry and the infallible identification littering up the evidence. Steinberg seemed rather smug about the whole thing. I decided to give him Gotham, much (I thought) as Pilate had given them Barabbas.

"Really," I said. "What time was the old Dancer turned up this morning?"

"Well, we found it around eleven. But we'd had a man in the garage all morning."

"Fascinating," I said, trying to look mysterious. "Who do you suppose is the invisible man?"

"Invisible man?" Steinberg didn't seem to see what I was getting at.

"Yes. There must have been one. After all, I saw the Mud Dancer myself this morning. It was upstairs, back in Gotham's apartment. Who do you supposed slipped it into the Wilsons' garage?"

That set him back a bit, I can tell you. His color changed from its normal ruddy red to a rather exotic shade of scarlet.

"You were in Gotham's apartment again this morning?"

"Well, yes. It occurred to me that a little chitchat about this and that might be in order. Didn't amount to much, though. I noticed the Mud Dancer was back, and the lights more or less went out. A friend of his hit me, then I think they must have given me a shot of some kind. I only just woke up."

"Did you call the police?"

"He didn't have time," Marie broke in, saving me a bit of embarrassment. "He'd only just woken up when I got here; we figured out what had happened; then you arrived."

Good girl, I thought. It was beginning to sound as if I wouldn't notify the authorities if the building burnt down. I decided to put in a good word for me. "You might say I'm reporting the incident now."

"Feel like going up there again?"

"Again?"

"I thought you and I might take a little walk up there. This character Gotham sounds interesting."

"I can assure you, he's not," I said, completely missing the point. But then, I've missed a point before, and I'll probably miss a point again.

Steinberg, in his policemanlike manner, spelled it out for me.

"I mean I'd like to ask him some questions."

"And you want me to go along?"

"I think so. It's usually harder for someone to claim total innocence if the victim is right there."

I agreed reluctantly. Not that I didn't want to see this Gotham brought to justice. I just didn't want to see Gotham personally. However, when one is in trouble with the law, it's generally best to do what the law suggests. Shows the old spirit of cooperation, and all that. So off we went.

Steinberg pressed the bell, and there was a long silence. I felt easier, and he pressed it again. Another long silence, and it began to look as if I wasn't going to have to see the man, after all. Things perked up in my personal world.

"Still got your keys?" Steinberg asked. Things perked down again.

"Wouldn't that be a little bit, um, illegal?" I asked.

"Only if we get caught."

It seemed a rather fast and loose attitude on the part of Beverly Hills's finest, but on the other hand it was also somewhat unarguable. I produced the keys, and in a trice we had made our entry.

Nothing much had changed in the place, except that the Mud Dancer was no longer on the coffee table. Nor did it turn up in the cabinet. I thought that was odd, until I remembered that it was now at the Beverly Hills police department. Then it no longer seemed odd at all.

"Well," I said, a little too brightly, if truth be known, "it doesn't seem to be here, does it? Shall we go?"

"Not so fast. Let's have a look around."

Steinberg marched down the hall toward the kitchen, and I stayed put in the living room. It didn't really seem to me to be my place to conduct an unauthorized search of the premises. If Steinberg wanted to do it, that was up to him. For my part, I would sit quietly and wait for the return of my host.

Steinberg slid through again and disappeared into the dressing room. I heard him clump through the bathroom, then head for the bedroom. He was back in a moment.

"Find anything?"

"Mmm-hmm. Where's the phone?"

I pointed it out on a table near the front door. "Not the Mud Dancer, I hope?"

"No. Not the Mud Dancer." He started dialing, then spoke into the phone. "Bill? Steinberg here. I'm at Ninth and Hobart. Better call L.A. Homicide. We seem to have another one. That's right. I'll be here." He hung up.

"Oh, my God. He's dead?"

"That's right. You want to take a look, Mr. Brett? I need a positive identification."

I didn't want to take a look. I didn't want to take a look at all. Bodies depress me, and, having seen Harry that morning, I rather thought I'd filled my quota for the day. That, however, didn't seem to be the case. I only hoped old Gotham's wig hadn't come off. Without it, I probably couldn't make the positive identification required. Dutifully, if reluctantly, I followed Steinberg into the bedroom.

"Is that Gotham?" Steinberg asked.

I looked. It wasn't. "No. It's the other one. I don't know what his name is. Gotham called him Troy. He's the one who hit me."

It struck me that the fellow had gotten everything he had coming to him. I mean, people who go about hitting other people deserve to be hit themselves once in a while. Although this did seem a bit drastic. I mean, I'm all for the punishment fitting the crime, and, after all, this Troy person hadn't killed me. It didn't, however, appear that he was going to wake up after the allotted twelve hours he owed me. Somebody seemed to have overcompensated.

"What happened?" I asked. I was, of course, obvious. He'd been done in. But I wanted some specifics.

"Shot through the head." Well, that was specific.

"That's odd. I didn't hear anything." Steinberg gave me what could only be called a withering look. I wondered about it, till I remembered that I hadn't been my usual alert self through most of the day.

"Oh," I said, recovering, "I wouldn't have heard anything, would I?"

"Not that you would have done anything about it if you had," Steinberg muttered.

That, I thought, was grossly unfair of him. Obviously, the man had the impression that I was one of those citizens who are chronically remiss in their duties. The kind who don't vote, among other things. I thought about making a snappy rejoinder to his criticism, but, what with one thing and another, all snappy rejoinders seemed to have deserted me. After considering, I decided to let the comment pass unnoticed.

It was about then that I heard the sirens approaching, so I asked for permission to leave. I got it. I got the distinct impression that Steinberg didn't want me around. Most annoying. I made my way back downstairs, wondering idly whether I was going to find Marie stretched out in my living room, with, perhaps, a knife stuck decoratively in her chest. It wouldn't have surprised me; it had been one of those days. Instead, I found that she had fixed us another drink.

"Where's Steinberg?" she asked as I came in.

"Upstairs, tending to the body."

"Oh, no. Gotham?"

"No, his friend. Seems to have gotten shot through the head."

"But . . ."

"Pity, really. Not that I liked the fellow, but still, it's too bad, isn't it?"

"John, they'll blame you!"

Her eyes were wide open, and she seemed to be staring at me as one normally stares at a dog that has just committed an unmentionable on one's maiden aunt.

"Well, I don't see why. After all, I was unconscious all day. It's really rather hard to handle a gun with any degree of accuracy when one is out cold a floor below the intended victim." My irrefutable logic didn't seem to impress her.

"But who can prove you were unconscious?"

I thought about it a moment and realized that the chances were slim indeed that anyone had happened in on me and taken time-stamped photos. The thought crossed my mind that now might be an ideal time to take an extended hiking trip through the High Sierras. Marie seemed to read my mind.

"Is there someplace you can go?"

"Oh, I suppose if I wanted to, I could do some sort of vanishing act. But that would make me look rather guilty, wouldn't it?"

"You look rather guilty anyway."

"Perhaps. But they don't have a weapon yet, and unless someone's managed to smuggle a gun in here unbeknownst to me, they aren't going to find any weapons here."

I think it hit both of us at the same time that it would have been very easy for someone to do exactly what I had just suggested. We began a systematic search of the premises. Fortunately, no gun. We did, however, discover that the gin was still holding up. Another toddy seemed to be in order.

Steinberg reappeared, this time with a couple of uniformed officers.

"Mr. Brett?"

"Come in, Sergeant, and do bring the storm troopers with you. Still on duty?"

Steinberg smiled. A rather revolting sight, really; his teeth left a good deal to be desired. In that respect, he reminded me of home.

"Technically, no. But I wonder . . . would you mind if I had my men search the place?"

I smiled then and hoped my caps put him to shame.

"Not at all. But it isn't here."

"What isn't?"

"The gun. Marie and I realized someone could have planted it on the premises, so we've aleady searched. No one did. Plant it on the premises, I mean."

"Then you won't mind if they look around?"

"Not at all. Will you have a drink while the treasure hunt progresses?"

"Well . . ."

"I'll tell you what. I won't tell about your drink, if you don't tell about my keys."

Steinberg chuckled. I mean, he really chuckled. One of those throaty ones. You know? The kind that start way back and almost choke before they get to the surface. I've noticed that that particular kind of chuckle is usually to be found among people who don't chuckle much. Consequently, I felt pleased at having elicited one.

"Good. May I sit down?"

"Do."

I stirred up another drink, depleting the gin supply a bit drasticaly, and the bluecoats began their snooping.

"It's all very strange, isn't it?" I said, giving Steinberg his drink.

"Hmm?"

"These murders, I mean."

"Murder's usually strange, till you know what happened."

"Well, yes. But what I mean is, there doesn't seem to be much relation between old Harry and this Troy fellow. I could understand it better if we'd found Gotham up there."

"Oh? Why is that?"

"Well, what with his having been out at the Wilsons' yesterday, and having stolen the icon, and all that. He would seem to have been a more logical victim."

"Not necessarily. Murder isn't always logical."

I had the distinct feeling we were about to be let in for a discourse on the philosophy of murder. I wonder if they teach a course on it in the police academies. It would probably involve long papers with such titles as "The Knife Wound: A Study in Depth" or "Marriage: Motive for Murder?" The idea of the embryonic fuzz writing colonnated term papers bored me silly. It looked as if Steinberg was about to bore me even further. I was right.

"Murder usually starts out as a logical entity in the mind of the murderer. He thinks, 'I could kill him.' Then he realizes he really could. Then he starts figuring out how and usually comes up with a plan. But the plan seldom works. Eventually, there's a slip. Sometimes it's an elemental slip, like the body being found. You'd be surprised how many murderers bank on the body never being found. Or somebody inadvertently witnesses the deed. Like this case. Suppose you hadn't seen it happen? What would we have to go on? Nothing. But you saw it, so at least we know that the murderer was driving Mrs. Wilson's car. A beginning."

"But not an end?"

Steinberg smiled and sipped his drink. I hate people who smile and sip drinks. A repulsive habit that should be stamped out by legislation.

"No, not an end. Unless we can prove that no one could have been driving Mrs. Wilson's car but Mrs. Wilson. And that wouldn't be easy to prove. But anyway, it was a slip, letting the murder be witnessed."

"But what about the one upstairs? Was that a slip, too?"

"Could have been. Could be the young man knew what had happened and might have talked. Maybe he tried blackmail, and whoever killed him did it on the theory that another murder was cheaper than paying off. After all, you can only be put in the gas chamber once. Or maybe the two murders aren't related at all.

"What a charming thought," Marie put in.

It wasn't at all. I had a sudden vision of everyone I knew being involved in a series of unrelated murders, killing each other off like flies, with me right in the middle of everything, trying to prove that I didn't have anything to do with anything. Returning to London would have been a pleasure by comparison. Steinberg gave me a little relief.

"That's unlikely, of course."

I felt much better.

"Brett, tell me more about this Gotham character."

"I don't know much, really. He's a decorator, and he seems to have a steady stream of young men in and out of the place, and he isn't here much of the time. Never has any guests that I've noticed. Usually drives up, goes in, then comes out again and takes off. Edie can tell you more than I can. She'd called him in about Harry's study."

He turned to Marie.

"Did you meet him?"

"Only briefly. I was cleaning the study when Mrs. Wilson brought him in. She introduced us and mentioned that he was going to redo the room. That was odd."

"Odd?"

"Yes. You see, Mr. Wilson had just mentioned to me the other day how much he liked his study. So it seemed odd that Mrs. Wilson would have it redone."

"Where was the icon?"

"In a glass case behind his desk."

"Locked?"

"I don't think so."

"Do you know where the icon came from?"

"I haven't any idea. It was a fake, you know."

Steinberg straightened up. "A fake?"

"Yes. I was a little surprised that Mrs. Wilson didn't know. But I'm sure Mr. Wilson did."

"Then that's why he didn't report the theft to us."

"Why?"

Steinberg positively grinned. "How would it look if it got out that a collector like Wilson had collected a fake?"

"But if that's it, why did they even want it back? Why not just get another one?"

"That, young lady, is a question I would like to have answered. I guess Mrs. Wilson may have to talk a little more."

He finished his drink just as the blue boys finished their search. He got up to leave.

"Mr. Brett, I'll probably be wanting to talk to you in the morning."

"I'll be here," I said, "I hope." They left, and I turned to Marie.

"Another drink, or do you have to go, too?" She smiled at me, and I was very glad she didn't have a drink to sip.

"This is my night off." My eyebrows went up, and I wondered if I got her implication correctly. Her eyebrows went up, and I gathered I did.

"Should you, ah . . ."

"Phone Mrs. Wilson? It would be polite, wouldn't it?"

"Well . . . yes." She phoned Edie, and I was glad she said only that she was spending the night with a friend, leaving such things as name and sex to Edie's imagination. Come to think of it, Edie's imagination probably came to the right conclusions.

We had another drink or two and managed to stay off the subject of murder. We stayed on the subject of Marie, and I must say I learned quite a bit about her that night. Marie was a remarkable girl.

Eventually, the gin ran out, so we were forced to retire to bed. I must confess, I fiddled with a bit more than her buttons.

Neither of us got murdered that night. Better things happened.

VII

Came the dawn, as it so often does, and I must say that had it not been for Marie's presence, I would have awakened depressed. It really is miraculous what the sight of a red-haired woman on the next pillow can do for a man. I toyed with the idea of staging a replay of some of the night's more exhilarating moments but settled for crawling to the bathroom.

Moments later, I was in the kitchen, cursing at the Chemex. It never ceases to amaze me that a coffeepot with only one piece total and nothing that moves can continue to make my life miserable. But then, I grew up with teapots, and that makes a difference. Fortunately Marie appeared, wearing my Bath-coat-of-many-colors (none of which matched her hair), and rescued me. Minutes later, the fresh-brewed nectar sloshed into the cups.

Ordinarily, a cup of coffee is not something I look bravely in the face each morning. Rather, it's a daily trial that I subject myself to under the heading of Going Native. I figure if the Americans can stand it, so can I. So far, I seem to be, but all the returns are not yet in. Perhaps when it comes time for me to take the final walking papers, I may yet be found with a moldering tea leaf buried in a back molar. Only time will tell.

At any rate, there we were, Marie and I, enjoying our morning libations, and I must say, despite the events of the previous day, all seemed right with the world.

I was mulling over this happy feeling, trying to decide where it all came from, when Marie broke the silence.

"I suppose I'd better be getting back."

"Back? But you're already here."

"To the Wilsons'. She'll need me to help with the funeral preparations."

Well, that put a damper on my mood. Apparently it was going to be simply another day of business as usual for Marie. I'd sort of hoped she might be in a holiday spirit and be thinking of leaving Edie alone to fend for herself. I expressed this position, and got nothing more than a smile for my trouble.

"Oh, John, it's a lovely idea, but I sort of feel guilty about leaving her alone last night."

"Oh, for God's sake, you're not her daughter, and she's not a cripple. I'll bet she had a whole mob in for a grief party last night."

"John!" She seemed genuinely shocked, so I backed off a bit.

"Well, I mean, I'm sure she wasn't alone. Edie has lots of friends, and I'm sure one or two flocked round."

"Yes, but even so, I should have been there. After all, I am the maid. . ."

"I'd almost forgotten. You aren't in the least maidlike."

"Thank you." She toasted me with coffee. With her, it was a charming gesture. With anybody else, it probably would have severed all diplomatic relations.

"Anyway, I know where everything is, and I know where she leaves things, and, well, I think I'd better get back."

"Well, if you must, you must." A silence fell, and more coffee was poured.

"What are you going to do today?"

I shrugged. I supposed I wasn't going to do much of anything but sit around and wait for a call from Steinberg.

"Not much, I guess." She gave me a look which made me feel that I'd said the wrong thing. "Is there something I should do?"

"Well, you might see if you can find out where Gotham went."

Now, that floored me. I mean, really. It seemed to me, and I still think I was right, that that particular job was best left to the police. That's what they're paid for, if you know what I mean. On the other hand, here was a perfectly charming girl, whom I really did want to impress, and it seemed as though a little amateur snooping on my part would impress her. I was stuck, obviously, on the horns of Damocles, or whatever that phrase is. At any rate, I was stuck. I gave it one more try before giving up.

"I should stay around here in case Steinberg calls."

Marie dismissed that notion in a couple of seconds. "You can call him and find out when or if he wants to see you. Then you can meet him at his office."

I had to admit that it seemed reasonable, so I agreed to go along with it.

"Very well. Where shall I start?"

That stopped her, but only for a moment.

"Call Edie, and find out where she got onto Gotham. Then go there."

The call was duly made: "Edie? John."

"John. I was just going to call you. Ask Marie how this damned coffeepot works, will you?" Her imagination, apparently, had come to quite correct conclusions. I got the required information and passed it on.

"Thanks, John. When will I be seeing you?"

"Well, I don't know, really. But I should think soon."

"Good. Well, thanks again. Bye."

"Edie, wait! I called you!"

"That's right, isn't it? Why?"

"I need to know where you found Gotham."

"I haven't found him at all. Is he gone?"

"No, no, no. I mean originally. But yes, he's gone."

"Where?"

"I don't know."

"Well, I'm sure I don't, either."

"Edie, just answer the question."

"Which one?"

"The one about where you got him."

"I didn't. Hans did."

"Hans? Who's Hans?"

"Hans von Berlin."

"Oh, now really, Edie. This isn't a joking matter."

"It isn't a joke. Hans von Berlin isn't his real name. It's his professional name. He has a salon on Robertson. I think his real name is Jimmy, but he changed it. Why?"

"Oh, I thought I'd go out and ask around a bit today and see what I can find out about your friend Gotham."

"What a marvelous idea. Marie must have suggested it."

"Yes."

"Marvelous girl, that Marie. I wish she'd stay on as my maid."

"I thought she was."

"I mean permanently. I think now that Harry's gone, I'm going to need some awfully good servants, just to keep track of me."

"Maybe Marie can help you find some."

"I hope so. Put her on a minute, will you, darling?"

I handed the phone to Marie, and the two of them conferred a minute. When she put the phone down, Marie stood up.

"I'd better get dressed."

"I rather like you that way."

She smiled. God, did she smile. "I know. But I have to get going. There's a lot to do." She headed toward the bedroom.

While she dressed, I called Steinberg and set up an appointment to see him that afternoon, then picked up the phone book. It was true. There *was* a Hans von Berlin listed on Robertson Boulevard. I hadn't really thought there would be.

Marie moved into the bathroom, and I took over the bedroom. Then we traded off and somehow both managed to be ready at the same time. I gave her one more kiss for good measure. It was a very good measure.

"By the way," I said as we left, "what's the fastest way to Four Hundred South Robertson?" I didn't see any point in getting lost.

"I always take Olympic. Too many lights on Wilshire, and they aren't synchronized." The girl was a veritable fount of information.

She climbed into her Mustang, which turned out to be the first thing about her I didn't like. It was an old model, but not old enough to have improved with age. But then, I don't suppose that on a maid's salary she was exactly in a Ferrari bracket. But even so, well, a Mustang? Just not proper. Not proper at all. I mean, compared to that Mustang, my Sunbeam was a Rolls-Royce. (People living on English hush money aren't in a Ferrari bracket, either, more's the pity.)

So off we went, dodging traffic and each other, toward the better parts of town. She was right. Olympic was faster. Not chic, but fast. I made a note to remember Olympic and filed it away in my brain. Who knows where it wound up.

I turned off at Robertson, and before I knew it, the four hundred block loomed up, complete with a rather odd-looking establishment with *Hans von Berlin* engraved in granite above the portcullis. (Not only a portcullis, but the name of the establishment was done in Old Germanic script, no less. I can tell you, I was impressed.) I parked the Sunbeam and began looking for the bellpull. It didn't occur to me that a place that looked like that would be open to the public. I was sure that one would have to pull a bellpull, then wait while the dogs were chained up and the deformed servant stashed away in a belfry somewhere.

No such thing. Just a discreet sign tucked away behind a potted pine tree that let the world know that Hans von Berlin was at home "to the trade only."

I pushed my way in anyway, on the assumption that if this was only the tradesman's entrance, I'd just as soon not see the front door. I was greeted by a rather icy-looking blonde, who stood a good five feet sitting down. I hoped she wouldn't stand up. I was still nursing something of a hangover, and she probably would have been a bit more than I was capable of bearing.

"Yes?" Her voice sounded less than friendly and distinctly German. Undoubtedly some sort of unreconstructed Nazi.

"I'd like to see von Berlin."

"You haff your tax cart?" I was momentarily baffled, but with me bafflement is always only a momentary thing, and I quickly figured out what she was getting at. I tried to bluff it through.

"Oh, no, dear girl. I don't even carry my passport with me."

She smiled, obviously pleased. "I'm sorry. This shop is not open to the general public."

"Good heavens, young lady. If you're not open, how can you make money?"

She tried to wither me and almost succeeded. "You don't understand, sir." She had me there, all right. "Ve only sell to decorators and retailers. If you don't haff a tax cart, you may not come in the store."

I decided to give the old Sunday pants ploy a whirl. "I left my card in another suit."

She nodded, apparently having heard that one before.

"Fine." I brightened. "If you're previously registered here, there will be no problem." I dimmed. I was just about to give it up, when a third party appeared.

"Good morning, Elsa," he fairly sang, deafening all those present. Then he noticed me. "Oh. Good morning, sir."

"This man doesn't haff a tax cart," Elsa announced, looking as pleased with herself as if she'd just discovered the true identity of Jack the Ripper.

"Oh?" The man turned to me. "I'm terribly sorry, sir, but we're strictly a wholesale house."

"The rabble's not allowed?" I said.

It took him aback. "Ah . . . well . . . it's not that, it's just that . . ."

"Excuse me," I broke in. "Are you Hans von Berlin?"

He recovered. "Why, yes . . ."

"Then you're the one I want to see. I don't really want to buy anything."

"Well, why didn't you say so?"

"Miss Buchenwald here wouldn't let me get a word in edgewise. She has a fixation about what she calls a 'tax cart.'"

She glared, but glares from receptionists just don't faze me anymore. Over the years, I've grown quite used to them. I've been glared at by some of the best receptionists in the world, and it hasn't gotten them anywhere.

"Mmm. Yes. Elsa, we'll be in my office."

We adjourned to the von Berlin inner sanctum, and I had a chance to look him over. Smallish, not over five nine, I'd say, and good-looking in an Aryan way. Predictably blond hair and eyes that would have been Danube-blue if the Danube were still blue, which it isn't. It's gotten to the point where, if you want to have Danube-blue eyes, they have to be brown. It's discouraging, but a lot of modern life is. Can you imagine someone bothering to write the "Brown Danube Waltz?" I can't. But getting back to von Berlin, he was nattily turned out in a double-breasted, flare-bottomed suit dyed to match his eyes, with a repulsive paisley handkerchief stuffed in his breast pocket. I had the horrible feeling that I'd run up against someone who was Now, if not Trendy. His office seemed to bear out my feeling. Lots of useless-looking white plastic furniture, set off by brightly colored accent pieces. There was an all-blue canvas mounted in a window frame, labeled "View from the Skylight—$1,250." The price of blue paint must have gone up.

"I don't believe I got your name, Mr.—?"

"Brett. John Brett. Interesting place you've got here."

"Do you like it?" he said a bit smugly.

"I said it was interesting. Not my taste, I'm afraid."

He looked crestfallen. "I think it's all very Now," he said.

"Oh, yes. Trendy. Very Trendy." I can use the lingo, too, if I must. "Personally, I prefer things a bit more traditional. You know, nice warm naugahyde, in peacock blue and tangerine."

"How terribly nineteen fifties," he said, managing only the weakest of smiles. I thought about twisting the knife a little more but decided to drop it. He probably wouldn't have caught on, unless I'd told him my favorite color was Doris Day yellow. No one *ever* takes that seriously. It looked like a good time to get on to business.

"Actually, von Berlin, I'm hoping you can give me some information."

"Information?"

"Yes. I'm a friend of Edith Wilson's."

"Oh, Edie. Wonderful woman, Edie. How is she?"

I decided I'd let him read about it in the papers. "Fine. But she told me you might know where I could find someone."

"Oh?"

"Yes. His name's Gotham."

"Harry Gotham?"

"Probably. I don't know his first name. He's a decorator. Edie'd asked him to do Harry's study over."

"Yes, that's Harry Gotham. I recommended him to her. An odd sort of fellow, but quite good. He's very big on primitive art, so I thought he'd fit in well with the Wilsons' scheme of things. Did Edie like him?"

"Oh, yes. Quite pleased. Quite pleased, indeed. But we seem to be having some trouble getting hold of him."

Von Berlin nodded. "Mmm-hmm. That's Gotham, all right. He disappears now and then. He's got a place up in the mountains somewhere. I think he likes to go up there by himself sometimes. I don't know, really. Like I said, he's an odd sort, and I don't know him too well."

"Do you know anybody who does?"

"Why? Is there something wrong?"

"That's what I'm trying to find out. He's not home, and Edie hasn't been able to reach him for a couple of days."

"Well, I don't know where you might find him."

I was about to give the whole thing up as not being worth the time, when the man seemed to come up with an idea.

"Wait!" Well, I hadn't been going anywhere, and "Wait!" seemed a fatuous thing to say, but I did my best to give an appearance of waiting.

"There is someone who might know. He works up the street in a yardage store."

That was all I needed, I thought. I could spend the rest of the day wading around in piles of orlon and dacron, with assorted furs and pelts thrown in for good measure, trying to find out the location of the country residence of a rather "odd" decorator. The prospect, I might say, did not thrill. I was about to tell him to forget it—it probably didn't matter, anyway, but the man was irrepressible. I've noticed that about Germans; you can't keep them down. No matter what, there they are, always in there pitching. (Rather like us English, come to think of it, but at least we don't bat about yelling, "Wait!" A simple "I say" usually suffices.)

"It's right up the street. Kauffman's. They have a boy there who knows Gotham. His name's Troy."

I considered telling him of the recent demise of this Troy fellow but decided he might just as well read about that in the papers, too. No one likes the bearer of ill tidings, as I believe someone once said.

"Troy, you say? That's an unlikely sounding name."

Von Berlin nodded. "Yes. Well, he probably made it up. On this street, we're worse than movie stars."

"Isn't Hans von Berlin your real name?"

"Not likely. It's really Jimmy Kepplemeyer, and I'm from Tarzana. But how can Jimmy Kepplemeyer from Tarzana run a place like this? It would be camp!"

It struck me that the whole thing was pretty camp, anyway, but I thought it best not to mention it. Instead I faded away. As I walked past Elsa, I thought I heard her mutter something. It sounded like: "In the Fatherland, people without tax carts vere taken avay!" but I'm sure I couldn't have heard it right.

Reluctantly, I made my way up the street to the Kauffman establishment on the theory that I had some time to kill, and Marie would certainly have words for me if she found out I hadn't traced all leads to the bitter end. With luck, I thought, no one at Kauffman's will know anything about anything. No luck.

Kauffman's turned out to be run by an old Jewish man and his wife. When I mentioned where I'd been, he made me like him at once.

"Hans von Berlin!" His eyes rolled back. "A nice boy, even if he dresses funny. But that girl! Oy! Elsa, she's calls herself. Don't you believe it! She's Eva Braun with a face lift."

"Joel! That's a terrible thing to say. Don't you believe him. He's only saying that to try to shock you." She went off, shaking her head.

Kauffman's head fell back, and his laugh almost deluged us with the piles of material that filled the place.

"I only say that to shock *her.* Not you. Never shock the customers, that's my motto. Were you shocked?" He suddenly looked alarmed.

"Well, no, not really."

Kauffman came back to life. "Good. It's all right, then. Rachel's a good woman, and I love her, but it's fun to give her a jolt every now and then. That's another of my mottos. What can I do for you?"

"I understand you had a fellow working here named Troy."

"That's not his for-real name."

"So I'm told."

"Around here everyone changes their names. Everybody's got to be somebody. And all so they can raise the price of a chair. If I was smart, I'd change my name to René de Paris and double my profit margin. But who would believe it?"

"About this fellow Troy. . ."

"Yah. What about him? He's late again. Always late. Stays up all night doing God knows what and can't get to work in the morning. If I paid him a decent wage, I'd fire him, but what can you do? I ask you, what can you do?"

"Well, I'm afraid you can't fire him."

"Oh, can't I? Just watch me." Then he turned suspicious. "You from the labor board? I pay the minimum."

"No, I'm just looking for information."

"Information's cheap. What do you mean, I can't fire him? I hired him, I can fire him. If Rachel says I can."

"I'm terribly sorry, Mr. Kauffman, but I'm afraid you can't. He got himself killed last night."

His eyes popped out, and it looked for a moment as though, in addition to my current problems, I was about to have a cardiac case develop before my very eyes. He sort of clawed, doglike, at the air, and strange sounds emanated from his throat. His face turned purple, which went very well against the black velour that happened to be behind him. Created a sort of royal effect and made me feel at home.

"Rachel!" he croaked. "Raaachel!"

The woman bustled out of the back. "Joel? Is that you, Joel?" Then she saw him. "Young man, what have you done to my Joel?"

Kauffman looked to be on the edge of expiring, his hands still churning about in the atmosphere.

"That Troy," he sputtered. "Rachel, do you know what that worthless kid has done now? He's gotten himself killed!"

"What?" Rachel looked back and forth at the two of us, trying to figure out what the confusion and excitement was all about. "What do you mean, Troy's gotten himself killed? Who would want to do a thing like that?" She shook her head, as if by the shaking all things unpleasant would disappear. I must try it myself sometime.

"No, ma'am," I said, attempting to put things straight, or at least straighter. "He didn't get himself killed. He got killed. I'm sure he didn't intend it. People so seldom do anymore. But he is dead."

"Gotham!" She fairly spat the name. "I'll bet it was that Gotham!"

Well, she wasn't going to get me to bet against her. I would have put fairly good odds on Gotham myself, given the opportunity. Unfortunately, the opportunity wasn't arising. Gotham seemed to have the field pretty much to himself in the Troy case.

"Now, now, now, Rachel," Kauffman said. "That's not a nice thing to say at all."

Suddenly they had changed roles. It was really a remarkable thing to see. All of a sudden he was calmed down, and her eyeballs seemed headed for the opposite wall. Also, she had taken over the windmill chores, which I thought was decent of her.

"Nice thing! Don't talk to me about nice things! I know that Gotham, and he did it!"

"You know Gotham?" I thought I saw a chance to get at the nub of things, and getting at nubs, I've found, is often helpful.

"You bet I know him. I know him better than I want to. If it was up to me, he wouldn't buy so much as a spool of thread here!"

"Why don't you sit down and tell me about it?" She didn't sit down, but she did tell me.

"That Troy! He was all right, till he met Gotham. And it wasn't the first time, either. Every time a boy meets that Gotham, he turns bad. Thinks he doesn't have to work no more. Like suddenly he's a king, or something!" It struck me that she had the rank right, but the gender wrong.

"I told him, but he wouldn't listen to me. 'Watch out,' I said, 'nothing ever comes from knowing Harry Gotham. Nothing good, anyway.' But he didn't care. All he cared about was the fancy clothes, and the fancy car, and the fancy restaurants. 'But what about next month?' I said. 'What about when he gets tired of you? I've seen it before, and I'll see it again' I said. But oh, no! He thought he had it made. And now look. Dead. You mark my words. Harry Gotham did it, but nobody'll ever prove it!" She turned to Kauffman. "Joel. No more. No more Harry Gotham in this store! Do you hear me?"

Kauffman nodded.

"We run a nice place here, young man, don't we, Joel?"

Kauffman nodded again.

"And we don't want no trouble. So the next time Harry Gotham comes in here, you send him right on out again. Let him ruin someone else's stockboy next time."

She appeared to have finished, so I ventured a question. "Do you know where Gotham lives?"

Her eyes blazed. "You bet I do. I made Troy tell me. I told him I should know, in case I ever had to get hold of him. Troy. You couldn't pay me to get hold of Gotham!"

"Could I have the address?"

"Which one?"

"Is there more than one?" I said, as if I didn't know.

"I got two. One in town, one in the country. That Gotham has too much money, if you ask me. Two places to live! Who needs two places to live?"

"I think it's the country one I need."

"Just a minute. It's in the back." She went off to the office and returned a few seconds later.

"Here it is. Lompoc. Such a name for a town. But it's only a post office box and a phone number. Troy said it's a ranch. Some ranch, I'll bet. Joel, can you see Harry Gotham on a horse?"

Joel chose to ignore the question, which I felt was an admirable thing for Joel to do. All it could have accomplished was a discussion of decorators on horseback, and such a discussion seemed to me pointless.

"How well did you know Gotham?"

"Me? Not well. Just well enough not to like him." It seemed that there wasn't too much more to be gotten out of Mrs. Kauffman.

"He asked me a favor once, but I turned him down," she said, looking quite proud of the fact.

"A favor?"

"A favor. He came in here with one of his statues and wanted me to keep it for him."

"Why?"

"Why? How do I know why? I took one look at it and told him to get out of here. Broken, even, it was."

"Broken?"

"A toe missing. Ugly thing, even with the toe. Looked like mud. He claimed it was art. To me it was mud."

"When was this?"

"A week ago. Two. I don't know. I told him if he didn't want it, he should throw it away. That got to him. He didn't come in here again, and I was just as glad."

"But why did he want you to keep it for him?"

"How do I know why? He didn't say. Just asked if he could leave it here. Nuts, I said. You want it, you keep it. Nuts." She turned around and stamped off to her office.

"Did you see the statue, Mr. Kauffman?"

"Nah. First time I ever heard of it. She's a good woman, my Rachel, and I love her. But she never tells me anything."

"What did you think of Gotham?"

He shrugged. "What does anybody think of anybody else? His way isn't my way. So he should leave me alone, and I'll leave him alone. I don't like him, I don't dislike him. But Rachel's right on one thing. Ever since Troy met him, Troy didn't want to work. Not that Troy ever wanted to work."

It began to look as if I'd gotten about all I was going to get. I thanked Kauffman for the information and left.

Getting my bearings took a minute, what with being in new surroundings and all, but eventually I spotted the Sunbeam down the street.

I was headed for it, with all good intentions of taking myself out for a little mid-morning drink, when a store window caught my eye. It was filled with what Edie would have called icons, and some of them looked as if they might even fall under the classification of primitive art. I decided to have a look.

Normally, I'm not much of a one for poking around art shops. An opening of a show is usually my limit. Openings have the advantage generally of being well stocked with free booze and edibles. I assume the theory is that if you ply the rubes with food and sauce, they aren't likely to notice that the level of talent cluttering up the field right now is rather frighteningly low. Get a rich man crocked and you can sell him anything seems to be the *modus operandi*. Fortunately, I'm safe at these affairs. I can't afford any of the junk that's for sale, so it doesn't matter how crocked I get.

At any rate, since I only indulge in art for booze's sake, as it were, I don't know much about art. A lot about booze, but not much about art. With this in mind, I plunged into enemy territory.

The first encounter seemed encouraging. I was greeted by a pleasant-enough-looking young woman who I hoped wouldn't know much more than I did.

"May I help you?"

Not so much as a word about a tax card; I felt better already. "I hope so. I was looking in the window."

"Did you see something you liked?"

"I'm not sure."

She laughed. "I know what you mean. At first, most of it looks kind of frightening, but you get used to it. Can I show you something?"

"First, why don't you tell me what they all are?"

"I don't know. I only know some of the easier ones. Like the painted wood ones. Those are Hopi *kachinas*."

I decided to try a long shot. "Do you have any Guinean pieces?"

"Guinean?"

"Yes. You know, from New Guinea." I thought specifics might help.

"Well, I don't know. What in particular were you looking for?"

"How about a . . . um . . . well, a Mud Dancer?"

Her eyebrows went up. "A Mud Dancer? I don't know whether we have any or not. I'll have to call the owner."

"Oh, don't bother. It was just a whim."

"No bother. He's in back. I'll get him. Would you like a cup of coffee?" She poured me a cup, then went to the back. I could hear her talking.

"Mr. Hinman, there's someone out here asking for a Mud Dancer."

"Indeed?"

"I thought maybe you'd better talk to him."

"Yes, I suppose I'd better."

A moment later a rather imposing fellow appeared, tall, with rusty hair and horn-rimmed glasses. Professorial. That describes him. Definitely professorial.

"Good morning," he said. "May I help you?"

Then it hit me. "Good Lord, you must be Marie's uncle."

"Marie Kellerman?"

"You are, aren't you?"

He nodded. "I plead guilty. But how did you know?"

"She said her uncle was James Hinman. Your girl here called you Mr. Hinman, and when I saw you, well, the hair's a dead giveaway."

He smiled, and I was pleased to note that he had Marie's smile as well as her hair. Perhaps the day wasn't going to be all unpleasantness, after all.

"It is, isn't it. How do you know Marie?"

"Oh, I'm a friend of the Wilsons'."

"Ah. Pity about Mr. Wilson."

"Marie called you?"

"Yes, yesterday. I knew him quite well, you know. In fact, I sold him the Mud Dancer. I suppose that's why you're here."

"Actually, no. I was just passing by and saw your window, so I thought I'd stop in."

"I'm glad you did. I don't get to meet many of Marie's friends. You are a friend, aren't you?"

"I certainly hope so."

"Well, then. Sit down, and let's get acquainted. What did you want to know about a Mud Dancer?"

I sat down, all at sea. It occurred to me that I should probably ask some astute questions, but frankly I couldn't think of any. I settled for some dumb ones.

"I don't know. What do you know about them?" That struck me as pretty dumb, even for a beginner.

"Not a whole lot, I'm afraid. They're quite rare, of course, and highly illegal."

"The National Treasures Acts." I thought I'd throw in something to make me look good.

"Yes. The one I sold Wilson didn't have any papers, so I told him to be careful of it. I hadn't even shown it to anyone else."

Apparently he didn't know it was a fake.

"How did it get broken?"

"Broken?"

"Yes. There's a toe missing."

"It wasn't broken when I gave it to him. That's a shame. I wonder how it happened."

I began to wonder, too. The Wilsons weren't ones for breaking up their icons. "Well, those things do happen, don't they?" I tried to brush it off, not too successfully.

"Not with the Wilsons, they don't. I've never heard of them damaging anything before. They treat things better than museums."

"Yes. Well, we're not going to find out now, are we? I mean, what with Harry dead and all."

"No," said Hinman, "I don't suppose we are."

That subject finally seemed to be over. I decided to try him on another. "Do you know Harry Gotham?"

He looked at me. "Harry Gotham? I don't think so. Should I?"

"I don't know. He collects primitive art, so I thought you might."

He thought a moment. "I don't think so. I might, of course. I meet a lot of people, and I'm afraid I'm not much on names. You know how it is."

I didn't. I never forget names. It's about the only thing I never forget, but I never forget names. It's a redeeming quality. I'm told by those who know that

I don't have many of them, so I like to point them out when the opportunity arises.

"Yes, of course," I lied. Lying is not a redeeming quality, but I confess I do it occasionally. It covers a lot of otherwise awkward moments. Hinman seemed to be musing, so I drank my coffee and kept my mouth shut.

"Marie's cover must be broken," he said finally.

"Beg pardon?" The terminology escaped me.

"Excuse me. I'm given to spy stories. I mean, she must have told you that she really isn't a maid. Not a professional one, anyway."

"Oh. Yes. Edie thought she might want to quit as soon as the murder happened. Something about a blot on her record, I believe."

"So she owned up?"

"Yes. I think it gave Edie a jolt. I think she felt like she'd been had."

"Well, it won't last long. Marie told me she's going to stay on, and she can be a lot of help. She'll be much better for Mrs. Wilson than a real maid. Very capable girl, my niece."

"A bit of a knockout, too, if I may say so."

"Oh, you've noticed?"

"It's kind of hard to miss."

Hinman frowned. Not an unpleasant frown, but one of those other kind. Sort of put on, if you know what I mean.

"I suppose I ought to ask you if your intentions are honorable, but in this day and age, I don't suppose any intentions are considered dishonorable, are they?" He paused a moment, leaving what could only be called an uncomfortable silence. Then he picked it up again.

"Come to think of it, why should I worry about your intentions? I don't even know your name."

Well, I'd done it again. Just when I think everything's going rather swimmingly, I discover I've blown it in the first paragraph. I did my best to correct the situation, with much groveling and apologizing. Altogether, I'm afraid I made rather a fool of myself. Well, what can you do . . .

"I understand the police think Mrs. Wilson might have killed her husband," he said when my spectacle was over with.

"So it seems. They also think I might have been in what you Americans call 'cahoots' with her on the deal."

"Any truth to it?"

My assessment of the man dropped instantly. Whatever happened to the presumption of innocence, which is touted as a Great American Tradition? All of a sudden, I was supposed to defend myself! Most distressing, I can tell you. Most distressing, indeed. It seemed to me that the least everyone could do was assume that my purity matched that of the driven snow until I proved otherwise. Doubtless it wouldn't take me long, considering the state of my purity, but still, America is still supposed to be America. Granted, they don't want the poor and huddled masses cluttering up their shores anymore. They have poor and huddled masses of their own now. Aside from that, the Constitution is still in effect, as far as I know, and the Fourth of July, and Mother, and everything else American. Why not the presumption of innocence? I decided to assert myself.

"No one's proved anything," I said.

"Does that mean you did it?" he said.

That, I thought, was my cue to stomp out in a huff. I did so.

I was heading toward the Sunbeam once more, getting my dudgeon worked up into high gear, when I thought I saw a familiar head of hair. The closer I got, the more familiar it looked.

"Marie!" I called.

The head turned. I was right.

"John! There you are. I was looking for you. Where have you been?"

The thought crossed my mind that now was not the time to tell her. Instead, I invited her to lunch. She accepted. We went. I got drunk. It was all very nice.

VIII

During lunch, which for me consisted of several drinks and not much food, I attempted to apprise Marie of the facts as I now saw them. These were mainly to the effect that Harry Gotham was probably not the most likable fellow in town, and if it were up to me I'd convict him of having murdered Troy, or whatever his real name was, and have done with it. Marie seemed to agree with my basic outline of things, but she had a question that struck me as being fraught with meaning.

"What was Troy's real name?" was the fraught question.

"How would I know?" was my somewhat less than satisfactory answer.

She looked at me in a manner that was definitely lacking in respect. She chewed on her lip a moment, apparently mulling over something. Then she looked at me again. I grew uncomfortable.

"You mean you didn't ask?" I detected a note of something unpleasant in her voice. Pique, I think one might call it. Yes, she was definitely piqued.

"Why should I?"

Her pique turned into vexation, and my discomfort grew.

"Oh, John, you're impossible."

"Now, that's an unkind thing to say. Here I've been veritably straining myself all morning, gathering facts like fall leaves, and you accuse me of being impossible!"

"I'm sorry. It's just that it seems like one of the first things you would have asked the Kauffmans was what Troy's name really was."

"I suppose I might have, if I'd thought it mattered."

The facts, actually, were that I hadn't thought at all, but I saw no percentage in letting my stock with Marie slip any further than it already had. However, the bear was in the market and showed no signs of getting out.

"Of course it matters. If we know who Troy really was, we can find out everything about him."

"But Marie, my dear, I don't want to find out everything about him."

"Well, I should think you would. After all, he hit you over the head, didn't he?"

"I think he's been well punished for that."

"But don't you even want to find out why he hit you?"

"Not particularly."

"Good Lord! Don't you have any sense of . . . of curiosity?"

I thought about it and decided I didn't. "Not really, no. I'm sure the police can take care of it very well."

"And you, at the same time."

That made me straighten up, I must say. I suppose the gin had made me forget that I was caught, as it were, between two murders. Perhaps a little curiosity might be in order, after all. I equivocated.

"I suppose I could call the Kauffmans . . ."

"Good."

". . . if I had a dime."

Silently she handed me the dime, and silently I went to the phone. When I had gotten the information, I returned to the table. Marie seemed to have forgiven me.

"When do I get my dime back?"

"Whenever I happen to feel flush. Well, I found out."

"What was his name?"

"Calvin. No wonder he changed it."

"Calvin? Calvin what?"

"Calvin Gunman."

It seemed to hit her rather like a ton of bricks. I mean, she reeled back, turned pale and went through one of those routines such as I had just seen at the Kauffmans.

"I say, are you all right?"

She tried to pull herself together, but the effort wasn't entirely successful. Her eyes took on a rather hardish look. "That bastard!" she said, her voice shaking.

I gathered that she knew the young Gunman, but the reference to the matrimonial status of someone's parents remained a bit vague. "You knew him?"

She nodded. "John, you've got to help me find Harry Gotham. I want him found, do you hear me?"

Her voice began to rise, and it appeared that a scene was about to take place. I dislike scenes.

"Of course," I said in my most consoling tones. "But how did you know this Gunman fellow?"

"It's horrible. It's just too horrible." She began to cry, her face stuffed in a napkin.

I reached out to touch her hand, but she pulled away, shaking her head.

"No, John, please. Don't touch me for a minute. I'll be all right. I just have to get hold of myself."

We sat there for a few minutes, me feeling foolish, what with a girl sobbing into a handkerchief while I sat doing nothing and people beginning to stare. A waiter or two gave me a withering, disapproving look that waiters give when customers don't behave properly, but I ignored them. Finally, Marie took the napkin from her face and carefully folded it. She seemed to be holding herself together by sheer will power.

"I'm sorry," she said, biting her lip.

"Marie, who was he?"

She shook her head. "John, it's . . . it's too incredible. Calvin is . . . was . . . my brother." For a moment, I thought she wasn't going to make it, but she did. Admirable girl.

"Your brother?" It all seemed a bit obscure.

"Yes. I haven't seen him for—oh, I don't know. Probably ten years."

"But your name is Kellerman."

She nodded. "When my father died, my mother remarried. Almost immediately. I think she'd been having an affair with the man long before Father died. His name was Phil Gunman. I couldn't stand

him. I'm afraid I made life rather miserable for him
and Mother. Little girls are always rather partial to
their fathers, and I felt as if mine had been betrayed.
So I was nasty. I don't suppose I was being very fair.
Phil was probably very nice, but I didn't care. He
wasn't my father. Anyway, I made things so bad that
finally they had to do something. I went to live with
Uncle James. Phil eventually adopted Calvin. I
haven't seen any of them for years, except Mother.
She'd come and see me, but she didn't want Calvin
to see me. She was afraid I'd poison his mind about
Phil. I probably would have." She stopped a minute,
then shook her head. "Now this."

"How old was he?"

"Calvin? You saw him. He couldn't have been
more than eighteen."

"He looked older."

"Some people do."

"Gotham likes them young, doesn't he?"

"Good God, John, you don't think—"

"Don't you?"

"Well, I guess so. I just don't want to think that
about my own brother. John, you've got to help me
find Gotham. If it's the last thing I do, I'm going to
make him pay!"

I took care of the check, and we left. I didn't think
Marie was in any shape to drive, so we left her car in
the street and took the Sunbeam.

"I think I'd better take you home. It looks like
Edie might have to help you out now, instead of vice
versa."

"No. I want to go see Sergeant Steinberg with
you."

"That can wait. I'll call him from Edie's."

"No. We'll go. He'll probably want to talk to me, anyway, when he finds out who Calvin was."

I pointed the Sunbeam in a direction that seemed likely to get us somewhere near the Beverly Hills Police Department. It didn't. Instead, we wound up in a rather dismal place called Culver City that has a lot of strange-looking streets meeting at even stranger intersections. In Culver City, I discovered, nothing goes anywhere. Everything is coming from somewhere and seems to dissipate into nothingness. It's what astronomers are lately calling, with a re-markable lack of cheeriness, a Black Hole. Every-thing collapses into it, and damned little gets out again. I began to flounder, and I'm afraid that the sight of a half-crocked Englishman floundering in a Sunbeam with a rather dazzling redhead at his side was enough to make the day for the locals. Not that they lined the streets to cheer, mind you, but I noticed a certain mocking quality in the eye of the policeman who stopped us.

"Going somewhere?" he asked.

It struck me as a rather stupid question, as it must have been obvious to him that we were not. After all, he had just succeeded in following us in five complete circles.

"Beverly Hills Police Department?" said I, giving him the bright smile.

"Wrong town. Try again."

Well, I knew it was the wrong town, for God's sake. All I was trying to do was get it across to him that directions were needed. He was obviously dense. I tried again.

"We want to *go* to the Beverly Hills Police Department." I tried to wither him with a look this time. Take my word for it: don't ever try to wither a Culver City cop. They take it personally.

"Beverly Hills Police Department is in Beverly Hills, Mac," he said, a bit of impatience creeping in about the edges.

"You don't say," I said, matching him tone for tone.

We eyed each other, sizing one another up. I was, of course, at a disadvantage, being squinched down in the Sunbeam. Prudence being one of my virtues, if not precisely my middle name, I gave it up and looked away. I decided to fall back on another of my virtues. Meekness. When pressed, I can meek it with the best of them. I was pressed.

"Please, sir," I cravened. "Could you give us some directions?"

That hit him where he lived. For some reason, I've noticed, a policeman will usually give you a hand if he knows he's got you where he wants you. Either that or beat you bloody. Consequently, it has been my practice, when dealing with the law, to let them think they have me where they want me. (They usually do, anyway, if truth be known.) This minion of the law fell right into the pattern.

"Well," he smiled, turning all over jovial, "why didn't you say so?"

He proceeded to give me a complicated series of instructions that got us very quickly to Santa Monica. From there, Beverly Hills was but a short half-hour drive. We confronted Steinberg only an hour after the appointed time. For me, that's punctuality itself.

The good sergeant was dour. Perhaps he'd lost a clue, or whatever it is policemen lose. At any rate, the visage was definitely dour.

"You're late," he said, stating the obvious. "Been out turning up more bodies?"

I deigned to overlook this. It was, if I do say so myself, a rather good deign, as deigns go.

"I've been out working on the case, as a matter of fact."

"Oh, Lord. Couldn't you just stay at home and sip tea or something? Well, what did you find out?"

"For openers," I said, borrowing a phrase from some of my sporting friends, "I can tell you Troy's real name."

"Indeed?" He didn't seem impressed.

"Calvin Gunman." I waited for the look of respect to come into his eyes. It didn't. Instead, he opened a folder.

"Calvin *Charles* Gunman. Age eighteen. Employed by the Kauffman Fabric House, on Robertson Boulevard. Home address: Eight forty-two and a half Palm, West Hollywood," he read.

"Why, that's remarkable. How did you find that out?"

He looked at me for a moment, as though trying to make up his mind whether to tell me. Finally, he decided.

"Well, Mr. Brett, it wasn't easy. It involved hours of intense police investigation. We looked in his wallet."

If he expected that to deflate me, he was entirely correct. I'm afraid I felt a bit of a fool. I played my trump card. "He was Miss Kellerman's brother, you know."

That perked him up. Apparently he hadn't known. I felt much better.

"Your brother?"

Marie nodded.

"Can you identify him? We haven't been able to reach his family."

Marie shook her head to this one. "I don't think so. I haven't seen Calvin since he was a little boy. My stepfather adopted him, and I lived with my uncle. The family wasn't close."

"Would you mind taking a look, anyway?"

"Well . . ."

"I'm sorry to have to ask you, Miss Kellerman, but if you could do it, it would save the boy's mother a lot of trauma. And we've cleaned him up, so it's not too messy."

That rather turned me off, but Marie must have been shell-shocked by then. She didn't flinch. "All right, I'll try. But I can't guarantee anything. I just don't know whether I'll recognize him or not."

And so we went to the morgue. It wasn't nearly as grim as I'd imagined it. Rather cheerful, as a matter of fact, what with a bowl of daisies on the attendant's desk. I mean, it could have been worse. Just suppose the attendant had been partial to lilies.

We ambled down a corridor, with Steinberg checking numbers, and finally stopped. Steinberg pressed a button, and young Calvin hove into view, if hove is the right word for an emerging corpse. At any rate, he appeared, discreetly covered by a sheet. (I wonder, do they wash the sheets after each use, like in a hotel, or do the sheets just go from one corpse to another, being washed on alternate Saturday mornings? It's a point to ponder.)

Steinberg peeled the sheet back, and we got a look at the late if not great Troy, né Calvin, Gunman. I had to admit, he'd been a good-looking sort. If nothing else, one had to admire Gotham's taste. Marie studied the face for a long time.

Then Steinberg spoke. "Well, Miss Kellerman? Is that your brother?"

"I can't be absolutely positive, of course. But now that I've studied it, yes, it looks like Calvin's face." She was silent for a minute, then spoke again. "Odd, isn't it? He doesn't even look eighteen. Why do you suppose people always take on a younger look when they die? It happened to my grandmother, too. When she died, her face must have lost twenty years."

Steinberg pulled the sheet back into place, pressed the button again and Calvin exited into the wall. We exited down the hall.

Back in Steinberg's office, the sergeant began filling out some forms, legally identifying the body as Calvin and legally declaring Calvin as being no longer among those present. It occurred to me that if a mistake were being made, and through some set of circumstances too wild for me to comprehend Calvin were actually alive and well somewhere, he was going to be in for some rough times. Steinberg didn't appear to be the kind who would take kindly to being told he'd checked the wrong person out. However, it didn't seem likely to happen. On the other hand, lots of unlikely things seemed to have happened over the last couple of days, and I did wish Marie's identification of the dear departed had been a bit more positive. Steinberg, though, didn't seem to share my qualms. I suppose getting some sort of name for the body put a gold star in his Sunday school book.

When he finished with his formalities, we got back to subjects at hand. Namely, the untimely demise of Messrs. Wilson and Gunman. Steinberg opened the bidding.

"Well, Mr. Brett, if you did it, you did it well. So far, we haven't turned up anything but the Mud Dancer. Here."

He pulled open a drawer of his desk and produced a wooden box. He handed it to me, and I did what was expected. I opened it. Before me lay the Mud Dancer. Except that on closer examination, it turned out to be *a* Mud Dancer. Not *the* Mud Dancer.

"This is what you found in Edie's garage?"

"That's where it was. Tucked up in the rafters."

"Very nice. I wonder how much it's worth."

"Worth?"

"Yes. I understand the real Mud Dancer would be worth quite a lot. And if Marie's right when she says the real ones are gray all the way through, this one's real."

I handed Marie the box. She picked up the icon and looked it over. Then she nodded.

"This one's real. It isn't the one that was in Mr. Wilson's study. That one was definitely painted, and the white plaster showed on the broken toe. This one isn't painted. Look at the toe."

Steinberg took the statue and examined it. "Gray. All the way through. Then this isn't the one you took out of Gotham's apartment?"

"Absolutely not. I snatched the fake. I identified it by the broken toe, and it was definitely white underneath."

"Damn," was what Steinberg said, and I couldn't really blame him. I mean, there was his prime clue zipping right out the old window. He put the thing back in its box.

"So we're back to Start, aren't we?" He looked at me as if he expected me to help him out.

If he was back at Start, that was his problem, I thought. I wasn't back at Start, but I wasn't about to help him, not after the way he'd brushed off my detecting in the matter of Troy's real name. I thought a little discreet probing was in order.

"So it would seem," I said, drumming my fingers together *à la* Sherlock Holmes, "so it would seem. What about Gotham? Found him yet?"

Steinberg's eyes rolled skyward, and momentarily I hoped they might get stuck. They didn't, and another hope was dashed. That seems to happen to most of my best hopes.

"Not a trace. We've got his apartment staked out and his phone tapped and an all-points bulletin on him and his car. We'll get him. It's just a matter of time."

I couldn't see any percentage in mentioning the country estate in the northern provinces; he'd only have used the information to his own advantage and left me out in the cold. He was that kind of man. Perhaps Marie and I could take a Sunday drive to Lompoc one of these first Sundays.

"What about Edie? Didn't you say you'd found her prints on the statue?"

"I said we'd found her prints. I didn't say on the statue. They were on the box. The statue's too rough to show a print."

"But that isn't the statue that's been romping around the neighborhood, so it doesn't make too much difference, does it?"

"No, not really." Steinberg seemed disappointed. "What's going to happen to it?"

"This one? I suppose we'll release it to Mrs. Wilson."

I saw my chance, and I pounced. "Why don't you give it to me? We're going out there, and I can give it to her."

Steinberg shook his head. "Not possible. Not unless you have a written authorization from Mrs. Wilson. Otherwise, she could sue us."

"Couldn't you call her?" Every now and then I like to play a long shot.

"No." So much for my pounce.

To make a long story short, we spent the next hour taking down my statements of what had happened. I even owned up to the theft of the statue, since neither the statue nor Gotham was around to make trouble for me, and Steinberg had said he wouldn't push the matter, anyway. Besides, I thought, I could always turn state's evidence, whatever that is. Sort of a Joe Valachi-west, if you know what I mean.

After the statements were taken, read and duly signed, Steinberg made some notes about Marie's relationship with her brother (nonexistent), and that was that. (I should clarify the parenthetical "nonexistent" in the previous sentence. I referred to the relationship, not the brother, although by this time, of course, the brother was nonexistent, too.)

By the time we were through with the B.H.P.D., or they were through with us, or whatever, the day was pretty well shot. We decided it was time to head Wilsonward, as it were.

Edie greeted us at the door, turned out rather spectacularly in black. Somehow, she rather bombed out in her role of grieving widow.

"Children!" she bellowed. "Where have you been? I've been frantic. Marie, I don't know where anything is, anything at all. All I could find to wear was this rag, and I'm afraid that, color aside, it just isn't very funereal. What do you think?"

Well, I'm not familiar with local graveside customs, but on the native soil, a respectable woman does not appear at her husband's funeral wearing a pants suit and wedgies, black or otherwise. I mean, it simply isn't done.

Marie concurred. "I'm terribly sorry we're so late, Mrs. Wilson. I'll find you some clothes right away."

"Nonsense. I've just ordered dinner sent in from Chasen's, since the staff [she looked pointedly at Marie] was out doing God knows what with family friends—mine, not the staff's—and I'll simply call them up and triple the order. Do you know, I heard they use a Cadillac Eldorado *station wagon* for deliveries? Now, that's what I call pretentious, if it's true. Where have you been?"

We filled her in, and she made nice sounds of sympathy when we told her of the relationship between Marie and Victim Two. On the whole, though, she seemed much more interested in the latest developments concerning the Mud Dancer.

"I told them," she said, after I finished. "Over and over I told them. I put that box up there myself, days ago."

I was aghast. "But didn't you know what was in it?"

"Of course I did, dummy. But who cared then? It was just a Mud Dancer."

"Didn't you look at it again after I called you when Harry got shot?"

"Why should I? I assumed Harry had gotten it down again, so I didn't even look."

"Why did you put it up there in the first place?"

She thought a minute. "Because Harry told me to," she said, as if that solved everything. Fortunately, the man from Chasen's arrived, and we had dinner.

IX

I think it was over the soup that it occurred to me
that I still didn't know much about Harry Wilson.
The soup was a mock turtle, and I don't know very
much about that, either. Perhaps that's how the connection was made. Be that as it may, however, it
struck me that a little background on Harry might
just be helpful. You never know what memories
from the past might turn up with gun in hand, as it
were. I probed.

"Tell me about Harry," I said, getting down to
what I think is called the nitty-gritty.

"What's to tell?"

"Oh, you know. Things that might be pertinent.
Enemies. That sort of thing."

"Jesus, John, you make this sound like a murder
mystery."

"Well, I mean, it is, rather, isn't it?"

Edie considered. Then she nodded. "Yes, I suppose it is, isn't it, unless one of us owns up to it, and
that isn't going to happen. Well. Harry. Yes. I might
as well begin at the beginning."

It seemed logical.

"Harry and I weren't always rich. Everybody thinks so, except those who knew. We're what is called *nouveau riche* behind our backs. Fortunately, we're *riche* enough so that nobody can do it to our faces. That makes it nice, don't you think? Harry came from Chicago. He was a lot different then—he made a small bundle during Prohibition, running decent booze in from Canada. Harry was funny about Prohibition. He didn't care if people drank or not, but he was all for Prohibition. He said if they legalized liquor, it would take all the profit out of it, and of course Harry had nothing against a profit. But then Roosevelt got in, and Hoover got out, and Harry saw the handwriting on the wall. So he cashed in his chips and came out here. Harry thought the Depression was the biggest business opportunity that ever hit. He kept looking around for people who were going under but wanted to postpone it for a while. Then he'd loan them some money, knowing perfectly well they wouldn't be able to pay it back, and wait a few months. Sure enough, they'd run out of cash, and Harry would foreclose. Then he'd find someone with some money, sell them the thing he'd just foreclosed, loan out the money to the next sucker and run through the whole routine again. Oh, I tell you, if you had a little money, the Depression made you rich. In Chicago they used to call it shylocking, but out here you keep your interest down and call it Savings and Loan. Everyone thinks you're doing them a favor while you clip them. But that's what makes the world go round, isn't it?

"Anyway, Harry got filthy rich and decided he should become respectable. So he married me, and looked around for something to do. That's when he decided to go in for the art thing. I took a few courses, but frankly, I'm not too bright, and I could never tell the difference between Monet and Manet, and Rembrandt and Raphael, and all those others. Harry could. Harry was smart. He got so he could eyeball a piece of art and tell you what it was worth on the open market or the black market, or at auction, to the nearest hundred dollars. And, in case you didn't know, with art that's close guessing. Anyway, we muddled along, and every now and then Harry would find a tax-deductible artist to support for a while, and pretty soon we were patrons of the arts. Then I got lucky. Warhol and Kleinholtz and that crowd came along, and suddenly you didn't have to know the difference between those Frenchmen and Italians anymore. I mean, let's face it—a soup can's a soup can, isn't it? So that's when my day started.

"Harry still had all the smarts, so he thought up the gallery-restaurant bit. Tax deductible again, and we could take all kinds of trips looking for new art. That's when the primitive thing started.

"You know, I think it was Harry's sense of adventure that really started that. The safari bit into the jungle, looking for masks and tapa cloths and all that crap. Harry never really got over the good old days in Chicago, when he could run around all night, making connections, rubbing shoulders with the Capone crowd, who really weren't so bad except that they liked shooting people, and generally being in the thick of things. Also, Harry was never one to turn down a profit, and the profits were nice in the booze business back then.

"Being rich and respectable sort of bored Harry. He always said the only difference between being rich and being poor was that being rich cost more, and instead of betting on a race, you fixed it. Of course, that's an exaggeration, but still, there's some truth in it, isn't there? I mean, what's really the difference between guzzling champagne and talking about Andy Warhol's soup cans, and drinking beer and talking about your favorite Campbell's? When you get right down to it, the soups are a lot more interesting than Andy's cans.

"Anyway, Harry got really interested in the primitive stuff. Particularly the icons. They were the only things around older than he was. He really dug those. He bought them and sold them just like real estate. I think a lot of the fun he got out of it was that so many of them weren't legal. He'd have them smuggled out of one country and into another, and double or triple the price to someone who wanted an illegal art treasure but didn't want to run the risk of getting it out themselves. I remember once we were in Greece or Sardinia or Turkey, or one of those places, I can't really tell the difference, can you? Anyway, Harry'd gotten hold of a piece of glass. Some sort of old bottle, all green and pitted, and the customs people got interested in it. You know what Harry told them? You won't believe this one. He told them it was a new Avon perfume bottle, made to look like a collector's item. Well, Jesus, I thought he'd had it that time. Ha! The sucker at the customs office believed him. That's another difference between being rich and being poor. When you're rich, they think you're honest. As if an honest man could get rich!

"Well, that's about it. Harry was rich, bright and bored. In a way, it's a pity Prohibition was repealed. Harry had a good time then. Oh, not that he didn't later, but he always said he was happiest then."

She looked over at me, and I'm afraid my mouth was rather hanging open. Edie seemed amused at the sight.

"Oh, John. I'm afraid I've shocked you, haven't I? That wasn't exactly the picture you had of Harry, was it?"

I did my best to put the self back together again. "Oh, ah, well, um, now that you mention it, you might say that there are certain aspects of Harry's life of which I wasn't aware."

Edie laughed. "I'll just bet. Certain aspects, huh? Most aspects would be more like it. Harry was pretty quiet about himself most of the time."

Marie finally stirred herself. "But Mrs. Wilson. Didn't anyone know about Harry's early life?"

"Of course, my dear. Everyone he met when he first came out here knew who he was and where he came from. But the richer you get, the less people talk about you. Right, John? You should know *all* about that, coming from England."

God knows, I knew. It was practically a rule of thumb: thou shalt not speak ill of the well bred. "Well bred," naturally, was measured by traceable generations and pounds-per-year of income, added together and divided, more or less, by the number of maiden aunts you had living in the country and raising dalmatians. The same system holds true here, I've noticed, except that there are generally more dollars and fewer generations. The Wilsons, though totally lacking in generations, had enough dollars stashed away to be counted as extremely well bred. I apprised Marie of the above. She, being a bright girl, understood. I was proud.

I began poking around in my mind, as I am wont to do, for a possible motive for Harry's late demise. It seemed to me that somewhere in Edie's story, a clue must lie buried. Perhaps in the past, leftover from the rumrunning days. It struck me as not unlikely that there might be an aging gangster lurking about, fulfilling a leftover contract for some gang of Prohibition thugs. I mean, those things used to happen, and it seemed to me that perhaps, if the contractor hadn't been too bright, he might just now be catching up with old Harry. I put the proposition to Edie.

"Good Lord, John," she said, treating me to one of her withering looks. "Whatever put an idea like that into your head? If there had ever been a 'contract,' as you so quaintly put it, on Harry, it would have been filled long ago. Those guys didn't mess around. The orders went out, and within a week or so the deed was done. Besides, the button would have to be Harry's age by now, and the mobsters that are still around by the time they get to be Harry's age are not, I can assure you, running around burning people. They're far too busy trying to balance their tax returns and avoid photographers from *People*."

I withered. It isn't my habit to wither, as was mentioned earlier with regard to the receptionist Elsa, but Edie wasn't a receptionist. Consequently, my standards did not apply.

"Well," I said, after I'd finished withering, "obviously Harry's dead, so obviously there has to be a motive."

"Brilliant," Edie said, pointing out the obvious.

"Thank you. Now, I propose that the motive had something to do with the Mud Dancer."

"You don't say," Edie said, again pointing out the obvious, since I had just said it.

"Tomorrow, Edie, you pick up the icon from the gendarmes, and we'll take it to Marie's uncle."

"Uncle James? Why?"

"Oh, I have my reasons," I said, trying to sound mysterious but succeeding only in sounding vacuous. Then I stood up. Standing up always gives one an air of taking a situation in hand. "I understand Gotham was going to redo Harry's study."

"That's right," Edie replied. "I thought it was time. I hadn't had the study done yet this year."

The reasoning was lost on me, but I let it pass. I'll never understand why some people have to have everything redone every year. Have traditional values all gone down the drain? Well . . .

"May I see the study?" I don't know why I felt it necessary to have a personal look at the place, but it seemed a good idea.

"You know where it is. Do you want us to come along?"

"Oh, no. Finish your wine." With a gesture meant to indicate male superiority in matters such as this, I left the room. I don't know whether the gesture indicated what it was intended to indicate, but it did succeed in smashing a perfectly good vase. Ming, if memory serves.

I found the study with no trouble, which isn't remarkable, really, when you consider I had probably been in it a hundred times before. However, I feel that in setting forth a chronicle such as this, it's best to give equal time to the easy parts, as well as to the hard parts. Besides, for me there simply aren't that many easy parts.

The study seemed no different. Full of bookcases and display cases, and Harry's desk and a couple of easy chairs (Morris variety, if anybody's interested), a piece of sculpture or two and a fireplace. The mantelpiece sported a built-in candelabrum at each end. Now, being an avid reader of what is called Gothic literature, I am well aware that if there is a secret passage in a room with a fireplace with built-in candelabra, the door to that secret passage is going to be opened by turning one of those candelabra. I made for the fireplace and clutched on, as it were.

Apparently old Harry read the same Gothic books I did. Sure enough, just as I'd planned, one of the bookcases retreated into the wall and slid to one side. Most sporting of it, I thought. The only problem then, of course, was what to do with the secret passage, now that I'd found it. After a few moments' careful thought, I decided to follow it.

Fortunately, it was not your everyday, garden-variety secret passage. I have a distinct aversion to ill-lit, crawly places that look as though they might jump out at you at any moment. This, however, was a passage of a different color. It had lights strategically placed every few feet and was rather nicely paneled in Philippine mahogany. It wouldn't have been my choice of woods, preferring, as I do, oak, but one can't be choosy when the secret passage is not one's own.

At any rate, the passage quickly descended the traditional flight of stairs, then headed straight off in the direction of what, under other circumstances, would have been the river. In this case, though, it was only the garage. A ladder went up the wall of the passage, and a simple push opened a trapdoor into what was a sort of large, permanently mounted storage box inside the garage. Very neat. Very neat, indeed.

I closed the trapdoor and made my way back to the house, musing on the way about the possible bearing my discovery might have on the crime at hand. It never occurred to me that the secret passage might have no bearing whatsoever.

I emerged back into the study and gave the candlestick the reverse twist, as was so often done by Bela Lugosi. Obediently, the bookcase slid back into place. And just as well, too, since Edie and Marie chose that moment to make an appearance.

"Finding anything?" Edie asked, looking as though she knew I wasn't.

"Mmmm," I said as noncommittally as possible.

"I doubt if you'll find the murder weapon, John," she said.

"You never know, you never know," I countered. "Are there any other ways out of here, besides the door?"

"Hardly. Unless there's a secret passage, or something like that."

"Well, there could be," I said.

"Oh, John," Marie put it. "You're beginning to sound silly."

I thought of showing them how silly I was, but then I got a better idea.

"Very well. I'll do my Houdini bit for you. Edie, are you sure there's no other way out of this room?"

Edie was beginning to look a little bored. "I'm positive. There's only the one door, and the windows are barred."

"Very well. If you ladies will go out for a minute and keep an eye on the door, I shall show you something. Leave me alone for, say, five minutes, then come back."

They left, and I leaped once more to the candlestick. A quick turn, and the door was open again, and I was inside. I found the button to press to close the bookcase from inside the passage and pressed it. The bookcase slid closed, and there I was, snug inside the passage. I had but to wait a few minutes, then press the button again and reappear in the study, wowing Edie and Marie. It promised to be a grand moment.

The only problem was that when the bookcase slid closed, it covered the release button. A problem. A definite problem. Obviously, I would have to make the miraculous reappearance through the garage. Then it struck me that it might be even more impressive if I went through the garage and back into the house, making my dramatic reappearance through the study door. Now that, I thought, would *really* be a moment to remember.

Unfortunately, the trapdoor was locked, too. Revolting. Utterly revolting. I sat down amidst the Philippine mahogany to think things over.

X

Under ordinary circumstances, one does not usually find John Brett thinking things over amongst the Philippine mahogany. However, it seemed that ordinary circumstances had been suspended for the duration, so I decided to make the best of it. (I might point out that when one is stuck in a secret passage with both ends locked up, there is little, if anything, to make the best of. On the other hand, one copes, doesn't one?)

What with thinking things over, and coping, and whatever else one does while in confinement, I passed a good deal of time. Exactly how much, I can't say. It seems that a clock had not been included in the general scheme of things when the aforementioned secret passage had been constructed. I whiled away a little time by imagining the scene above when Edie and Marie had returned to the study. Edie, no doubt, had noted that Mr. Brett was no longer among those present and gone on to more important matters, such as pouring a drink. Marie, I imagined, had been upset. She would, I assume, put in a little time as a search party of one, then, upon discovering that I had truly joined the ranks of the missing, would perhaps even go so far as to call the fire department. I wondered if secret passages were registered with fire departments. In the future, I must push for that. I'm sure it would save a lot of people undue worry. I mean, suppose one's maiden aunt who lives alone should turn up missing some day. One could quickly call the fire department to see if she had a secret passage registered, and if she didn't, one could at least stop fearing the old girl was locked away incognito somewhere, starving to death.

At any rate, I completed the scenario in my mind, with a dramatic ending in which a cast of at least a dozen Beverly Hills firemen, led by Marie, hacked their way through to me, albeit destroying the passage and one wall of old Harry's den in the process. I didn't think Harry would mind, though, what with his having had his Great Loan called and the old body foreclosed upon. Not much use for a den when one is dead, is there? The only hitch in the whole scene was that so far I had failed to hear any hackings from without. As a matter of fact, I didn't hear anything at all from without, hackings or otherwise.

Well, comes the time when a man of action must take action, and it appeared that my time had come. I began a detailed exploration of the passage. At first glance, and second glance, too, for that matter, it seemed a perfectly ordinary Philippine-mahogany-paneled secret passage. A hallway, one might say, from the house to the garage, undistinguished by distinguishing features, dull, in fact, in every detail.

It was along about the third glance, which was really a fine-tooth comb affair, that I noticed something peculiar. Some of the paneling seemed hollow. I'd been doing the old tap-tapping trick, which had never previously netted me anything more than the location of an occasional stud, when all of a sudden it was as if the wall spoke to me. It practically screamed, "I'm hollow!"

That heartened me. I mean, a distinguishing feature was at least a hope, if you follow me. I continued the tap-tapping, and eventually discovered that there were three places, each about a foot wide and three feet high, where the wall seemed to be something less than solid concrete behind the Philippine mahogany. I began a series of systematic pokings, pushings and pressings. Eventually, I discovered further that if I pressed very hard on the lower edge of the paneling, it would move in and the entire piece slide down. Behind the panels, each of them, was a medicine cabinet affair, the shelves all lined with small bottles filled with various powders and fluids. It struck me that Harry kept his patent medicines in a rather odd place.

I sniffed at the bottles, but being something less than an expert sniffer, I couldn't tell a thing. I considered using the tasting method but put it right out of mind. Poison, and all that, you know.

I had gone through two of the cabinets and was about to open the third when I felt a button. It was tucked away at the end of the bottom shelf nearest the house end of the passage. I knew at once what it was, of course, and pressed it. Then I closed the cabinet and started for the door. I was just about to give it a pull, figuring it would open this time, when it hit me that the front-door entrance would be better, after all. In a moment, I was under the garage. The buttom had worked, and the trap door was no longer locked.

In a flash, or at least a trice, I was out of the passage, the trapdoor was shut and I was in the garage. Another trice, or perhaps a flash, and I was out of the garage and on my way back to the house. A moment later found me at the door of the study, ready to make my dramatic re-entry.

I threw open the door and struck a pose, prepared for an ovation from the ladies.

"Well, look who's here," Edie said. "It's the return of the Phantom."

Marie was a bit better. She hurled herself upon me and gave me a kiss that rather more than made up for Edie's sarcasm.

"John, where were you? I looked all over, but there isn't any other way out."

"Obviously, there is," I said, trying to sound mysterious.

"Well, yes, but where? I couldn't find it."

"You don't read the right books." I thought an obscure remark was called for, and that seemed pretty obscure.

"Tell me."

Her look was so pleading, it was hard to resist. Nevertheless, discretion triumphed.

"Later," I said, giving her a look I hoped was meaningful.

"That means he doesn't want me to know how he did it," Edie put in. "John, I don't think you trust me. Have a drink."

I accepted the drink, feeling I needed one after my ordeal in the bowels of the earth. I felt rather like a returning coal miner, after having survived forty days in a cave-in with nothing but stagnant water to sustain me. I tried for a bedraggled look. I don't yet know whether or not I succeeded.

I sipped my drink and eyed Edie. "Don't you want to know how I did it, Edie?"

"Not particularly."

"I should think you'd be interested. After all, it's your house."

"Oh, very well. Tell me, John, how did you do it?"

"I don't think I'll tell you."

"I didn't think you would."

"Oh? Why not?"

"Oh, for God's sake, John. If you were going to tell me, you'd have told me right away. I suppose you found something, and now you're waiting for me to make a slip. You've decided I did it, haven't you?"

"You? No. But you have to admit, it's a possibility."

"Marie, show him out."

I hadn't counted on that. I'd just thought I'd throw a little bait and see if I got a nibble. Now she'd gone and grabbed the whole line and was pulling me overboard. I decided to retreat a bit.

"Now, now, now, Edie," I said in my most soothing tones, "no need to fly off the handle. I didn't say you did it. Why would you?"

She stared into her drink. "When you get right down to it, I can think of a couple of good reasons. But I didn't do it. I'm going to bed. If you decide to tell me how you did the disappearing act, write me a note. Marie, come help me find something decent to sleep in. Am I supposed to wear black to bed, too? God, this is all too boring!" She stomped out, drink in hand.

There was a silence while Marie and I watched the retreating figure. Marie broke it.

"Too boring! Not exactly the grieving widow, is she?"

"Edie? Women like her never grieve. It might make their makeup run."

"Is that all there is to her, John? Just makeup?"

I considered it. All things set equal, Edie *was* one of the prime supports of the cosmetics industry, but there had to be more to her than that. Probably, I just hadn't seen it.

"Oh, no," I said. "She's really quite a remarkable woman. I mean, how many women with her background end up where she is?"

"That's hardly to *her* credit. Where would she be if she hadn't married Harry Wilson?"

"Oh, God, Marie. Please, let's not play that one. It gets too terrible too fast. I remember a round of that in London: 'Where would Lady So-and-So be if . . .' Where she would have been 'if' shocked her husband so deeply that he divorced her, and she wound up exactly where she would have 'if.' So let's not play around with where or who Edie might have been. She *is* Edie, and she *is* here."

"Well, it seems to me she's remarkably unaffected by Mr. Wilson's death."

"No more unaffected than you seem to be by your brother's."

"That's different. I hardly knew him. After all, when you're as young as we were, ten years is a long time."

"Still, he was your brother."

"I suppose so. But that doesn't have anything to do with it, really. John, I want to ask you a question."

"Fire, as they say, away."

"Do you think she could have done it?"

"Of course, she could have, but that's not saying she did."

"Well, did she?"

"What do you think?"

"I don't know what to think."

"Precisely. So I propose we give up thinking until tomorrow."

"All right."

I decided a small good-night kiss was in order and proceeded to deliver such. It turned out to be a good deal larger than small, with several embellishments that are not a part of your standard good-night kiss. It was all quite satisfying.

I was putting myself back together again, tucking in shirt, fastening belt, that sort of thing, when Marie slid her arms around me again.

"John?"

"Mmmm?"

"How did you do it?"

"Do what?"

"The disappearing thing."

I looked into her eyes and was treated to a swim in a lavender pool. Most unusual, but most charming.

"How do you think I did it?"

"There must be another way out."

"Perceptive. Very perceptive."

"But where is it?"

For a second, I was half determined to show it to her, but I changed my mind again. Let her suffer, was my idea. Let her beg and plead. In dealings with women, I have discovered that it is often best to have something to offer them, rather as a bribe. I call it the "Now be good, and I'll tell you where the secret passage is" gambit. Of course, one has to keep coming up with something new, for if you don't occasionally come across with the goods, they stop believing in your integrity. Consequently, a steady supply of goodies is needed. I figured the secret passage would hold up until the next day and, with proper handling, until the funeral. Harry's, not Calvin's.

"All in good time, my love," I whispered in her ear, getting a rather large mass of her hair caught in my teeth.

We disentangled me, and I made my way out. For a moment I was tempted to take her with me, but again I changed my mind. Let her while the time away trying to figure out how I'd gotten out of the study. I fitted myself behind the wheel of the Sunbeam and drifted away.

By the time I got home, I was beginning to wish I'd purloined a bottle of Harry's medicine. I mean, there seemed to be so much of it, and it did, on reflection, seem a curious place to keep it.

I fixed myself a small drink and sat down to mull things over. I went back over the whole dismal affair, step by step, and tried to put the pieces together. It turned out to be a three-drink mull, and by the time I finished, I'm afraid I was rather in my cups.

XI

The phone jolted me awake rather early in the morning; tennish, if memory serves, which, in my case, it very rarely does. My memory has a way of taking alternate Thursdays and Sunday afternoons off. There is a rumor around that it lives in Pacoima and only comes in when I forward it bus fare, which I rarely do. However, it was tennish the next morning, as I recall, that the phone jolted me awake.

A brief skirmish followed, and a draw was declared. I was on the floor, but the phone was off the hook.

"Brett?" inquired a revoltingly crisp voice. It was one of those voices that gets up at dawn and does exercises in the shower, thus preparing itself to ruin everybody else's day.

"I'm not sure," I mumbled. "I haven't made a positive identification yet. If I turn out to be me, I'll call you back."

I dropped the receiver on the hook, rolled over and curled up to a night table, prepared to go back to sleep. Crisp voice called back.

"This is Sergeant Steinberg. Don't hang up. I've made the identification, and you're you."

"Oh. Was it a difficult identification?"

"Not really."

"How disappointing. What do you want?"

"Answers."

"So did Alice B. Toklas. Only Gertrude died. I think I'll do the same thing."

"Not yet. Can you come down here?"

"I doubt it. I doubt it very much. Send an emergency resuscitator, and then we'll talk about it."

"Mr. Brett, are you all right?"

"Who cares?"

"The Beverly Hills Police Department!"

"That won't keep me warm at night."

"Mr. Brett. . ."

"Oh, call me John. . ."

"Very well, John—"

"And what shall I call you?"

"Herbie. Now, John. . ."

"*Herbie! Her*bie?"

"What's wrong with Herbie?"

"Well, I don't know, really. What is wrong with it? I think it's a very nice name."

"Tell you what. Call me when you wake up."

"Why, certainly. Perhaps we can lunch."

I thought I heard a faint scream at the other end of the line, but then everything went dead. It was just as well, for my money.

I made my way into the bathroom for the ritual ablutions, then continued into the kitchen, pausing to peer out into the outside world. It was all very depressing, so I treated myself to a morning hair-of-the-hound. It was time to face Steinberg. I dragged the phone out from under the bed where it had been cringing and set to with the dial. Within ten minutes, I had reached the B.H.P.D.

"Sergeant Steinberg, please," I said in well-modulated tones.

"Who may I say is calling?"

"Say anyone you like—who knows? You might even get it right."

"Thank you, sir."

In a moment, Steinberg came on the line. "Is that you, John? From what the operator said, I figured it had to be."

"It is."

"Good. Now, just a couple of questions. How long does it take to drive from your place to the Wilsons'?"

"Depends on what route you use."

"Elaborate."

"If you go out Wilshire, it take from forty to forty-five minutes. Olympic is faster. Thirty to thirty-five."

"The night Wilson was shot, which route did you use?"

"Wilshire."

"Mmm-hmm!"

"What does that mean?"

"I think we have her."

"Who?"

"Mrs. Wilson."

"Oh, now really, Steinberg—"

"Call me Herbie."

"Herbie. That's ridiculous."

"Oh? The phone company finally got through checking the records. A phone call went out of the Wilsons' house that night. To a phone booth on Olympic Boulevard. Strange thing. The call went out right after your call went in. As if it had been relayed."

Well, that rather seemed to tear it. I mean, how do you dispute the phone company? It just isn't done. They might disconnect the world if the world calls them liars. Edie, was, so to speak, on the hook. Then I remembered my mullings of the night before.

"Herbie? May I ask a question or two?"

"Sure."

"Was an autopsy done on Harry Wilson?"

"Yes. All homicides are autopsied."

"Good. Do you have the results?"

"Right here."

"About Harry Wilson. Was there anything unusual found in him?"

"Not really. Traces of insulin. He was diabetic."

"What about Calvin Gunman?"

"Junkie."

"Oh?"

"Heavy. If he hadn't gotten shot, he probably would have O.D.'d within a year."

"O.D.'d?"

"Overdosed. Happens all the time. Horrible way to go. They usually know what they did just before they pass out. The trip gets too wild. They wind up with the strangest expressions on their faces."

"I can imagine. What was he on?"

"Cocaine. Why the curiosity?"

"Oh. Ah . . . just curious, actually."

"Just curious? Or do you know something we don't?"

"What could I possibly know?"

"That's a good question. I wish I could answer it."

"Well, I'll call you if I find anything."

"I doubt it. That's why we have subpoenas. Talk to you later, John."

He hung up, and I'm afraid I stood with the phone in my hand for a minute, wondering what to do. Visions of blue legions descending on Edie danced through my head. I decided I'd better get out there.

Marie greeted me with a cheery kiss. Not, perhaps, as glorious as the kiss of the night before, but a kiss is a kiss, and one is thankful for what one gets.

"Is Edie here?" I asked when she was finished.

"No, just me."

"Oh, my God. Have they come for her?"

Marie looked baffled. "Come for her? What are you talking about?"

"Edie. Have the police been here?"

"Not that I know of. She left about half an hour ago."

"Where was she going?"

"She didn't say. What's happened?"

"Horrible things, my dear, horrible things."

I filled her in on my conversation with Steinberg. And when I told her her brother had been an addict, her eyes hardened. Not a pretty sight.

"That Gotham. John, we've got to get him. I won't have a minute's peace until he's found."

"Now, you don't know that Gotham had anything to do with it."

"Of course he did. First he seduced Calvin, then put him on drugs."

"And shot him? It doesn't seem likely."

"Why not? Maybe Calvin threatened to turn him in to the police."

"Maybe. But it still doesn't seem likely that he'd shoot someone in his own apartment, then walk out, leaving the body."

Marie considered. Obviously, I had a point, but she was reluctant to accept it.

"It's hard to say what someone will do in the heat of passion."

"Heat of passion? My God, you sound like a sex manual. How delightful. What do you do in the heat of your passion?"

Her smile broke through. "You should know. Oh, all right. It doesn't seem likely Gotham would have shot Calvin in his own bedroom, I'll admit that. But he's in this, and we've got to find him."

I thought I'd take her mind off the subject for a moment, since I didn't have the vaguest notion of where Gotham might be and didn't feel like taking off for Lompoc right then.

"About my disappearance last night . . ."

"You're going to show me?"

"I thought I would. Come on."

We went to the study, and I invited her to study the room. Study the study, as it were. It always increases the drama when one has failed in the search and is then shown the secret. Besides, with Edie out, we had plenty of time.

Marie poked about, checking the bars on the windows, investigating corners, shoving at bookcases, running her fingers under the mantel and all that sort of thing. She even pulled up a corner of the rug to look for a trapdoor. Finally, she gave up.

"You hardly tried," I said.

"I knew it wasn't any use. I searched in here half the night last night and couldn't find anything. You couldn't have done it.

I walked to the fireplace and gave the candlestick a twist. The bookcase slid back right on cue.

"My God," Marie breathed. "Where does it go?"

"Come on, I'll show you." We went into the passage and down the stairs. I tapped until I found one of the hollow places. "Look," I said. I opened the panel to show her the bottles. Only there weren't any bottles. Just an empty cabinet. I tried the other two. Both empty. I'm afraid I groaned.

"What's wrong, John?"

"Last night, all three of these cabinets were full of little bottles. I think they had drugs in them, but I didn't take one. Now they're all gone."

"Let's look further. Maybe there's another cabinet." She started tapping along the wall. When she was almost to the garage, she stopped. "Here," she said. "This sounds hollow."

I went to the spot and pressed. Sure enough, it opened. Inside the cabinet, lined up neat as you please, were forty Mud Dancers. Each fake, each with a broken toe.

Well, that just about ruined the day right at the beginning. I mean, one extra Mud Dancer floating around was bad enough, but now, here we were, stuck with forty more, and God knew where it might stop. It gave one pause.

"Well, I'll be damned," I said, for lack of anything better.

"What on earth—" was Marie's equally inspired comment.

"It looks like we've come on to the whole damn ballet troop, doesn't it?"

"But . . . but . . . why?"

"Let's just heist one of these and troop on back upstairs. Then I'll tell you my theory."

I put the grab on one of the little uglies, and we proceeded to the study. I closed the panel behind us.

"All right, John," Marie said, fixing me with an intense look. "What's going on?"

"Just a minute. Let me have that thing."

She handed me the Mud Dancer, and it seemed lighter than the one I'd gotten out of Gotham's apartment, or the one I'd seen in Gotham's apartment the next morning. (I was no longer assuming those two were one and the same, on the theory that with forty-two present or accounted for, a forty-third did not seem at all unlikely.) I inspected the thing rather closely, then gave the old head a yank. Sure enough, it came off. I nodded sagely.

"Just as I thought."

"It's a bottle?"

"Rather. Or a flask." *Flask* seems a sager word than *bottle*.

"But what's it for?"

"Drugs, I should think. Last night those three other cabinets were filled with little bottles of some sort of liquid. Probably drugs."

Marie's eyes widened. "You mean the Wilsons were dealing in drugs? That's ridiculous."

"Is it? Harry didn't mind dealing in liquor when that was illegal. And from what Edie said last night, it was the kick he got out of doing something dangerous that he enjoyed, not the money. So it stands to reason that now he'd be dealing in drugs as a sort of hobby."

"I don't believe it." She paused. "So now what do we do?"

"I suppose I'd better call Steinberg. The whole thing's getting a bit too sticky."

"But what about Edie? Was she in on it, too?"

I shrugged. "I don't know. I don't think so. Or anyway, I don't want to think so. But on the other hand, someone took the stuff out of those three cabinets last night."

"But I was in this room most of the night, and no one came in."

"But eventually you went to bed. And this morning all those bottles are gone, and so is Edie."

Marie nodded. I went to the phone to call Steinberg, but the damn thing went off just as I got to it. I clutched at it, trying to remember which end to talk into.

"Hello? Hello?" I said, doing my imitation of a parrot.

"John? This is Edie. What are you doing there?"

"That's not the point. Why aren't you here?"

"I would be, but I've run into a snag. I'm under arrest."

"Good Lord. What happened?"

"I came down to pick up the Mud Dancer, and that repulsive Sergeant Steinberg put the clamps on me."

"Rather walked right into it, didn't you?"

"Rather, as you so nastily put it. Anyway, get my lawyer, and get me out of here."

"They think you killed Harry?"

"Of course they do, idiot. And that boy, too. It seems they've found the gun, and it's mine."

"I see."

"I don't. Anyway, it's going to take fifty thousand dollars to get me back in circulation. Call Armand, and tell him to get on it. Harry's funeral is this afternoon, and I've got to be there."

"All right. Is Steinberg there?"

"Where else would he be? Do you want to talk to him?"

"If it isn't too much trouble."

She cursed a couple of times, then Steinberg came on the line.

"Steinberg here." Concise. Very concise.

"Herbie? John."

"Christ. What the hell do you want?"

I chose to ignore his tone, it being early in the morning. "You'd better come over here, and bring that Mud Dancer with you."

"You find something?"

"You might say so."

"Care to tell me what it is?"

"Not really, no."

"I'll bust you for withholding evidence."

"That's nice. Up till now, it was going to be murder, as I recall."

"I might do that yet. We found the gun in a vacant lot on Olympic, and it belongs to Mrs. Wilson. But that doesn't mean she fired it. All in all, though, I think I can take her to court. I haven't decided about you yet."

"Come on over, and we'll talk about it."

"Where are you?"

"The Wilsons'."

"OK. See you in about ten minutes."

He hung up, and after Marie had found the number for me, I called Edie's lawyer. He groaned at the size of the bail but agreed to have Edie out posthaste.

Marie had coffee made by the time Steinberg showed up. He came in with the Mud Dancer in its box. Things were a little strained between us, if truth be known. He sat down.

"All right, Brett, out with it."

"I found this, this morning," I said, handing him the Mud Dancer Marie and I had brought up from the passage. He looked it over, then took out the Mud Dancer he had brought. He began comparing them.

"Fascinating. Exactly alike, except for the broken toe. White plaster on one, gray on the other. Where did you find this?"

"Downstairs."

"Downstairs? This is a two-story house with no basement. From here there is no downstairs."

"Oh, yes there is. And downstairs there are thirty-nine more Mud Dancers just like that one."

"You'd better show me."

I opened the passage and was treated to a rather stupified look on Steinberg's face.

"You've got to be kidding. A secret passage?"

"Why, Herbie, how perceptive of you."

"Shut up. Where does it go?"

"To the garage. And it has four cabinets in it, one of which is filled wth Mud Dancers. Looks like a gift shop."

"The other three?"

"Empty now."

"Now?"

"Last night they were filled with bottles that could have been drugs."

Steinberg nodded knowingly. Whenever someone nods knowingly in my direction, it usually means trouble. I braced myself, ready for the worst.

"Last night?" He breathed the words with a distinctive inaudibility. I got the feeling he was less than pleased with me. I tried the "lightly passing it off" gambit.

"Why, yes," I said, lightly passing it off, "that's when I found the passage, you know."

"Why, no," he said, not swallowing it, "I didn't know. Somehow, in the confusion, you must have forgotten to call me."

"I suppose I—" Then I got it. The worst for which I was braced, and I can tell you, I was in need of every piece of bracing available.

"Don't suppose, Brett!" he roared. "You aren't supposed to suppose. You aren't supposed to do anything, except keep the hell out of this whole damn thing! Do I make myself clear? Because if I don't, I can make myself clearer! How would you like to spend the rest of the month in jail? I can arrange it, you know. And I will, unless you give me your solemn oath not to do any more meddling and to keep me apprised of anything you happen to stumble across in that stupid bumbling way of yours. Do you understand? *Solemn oath!*"

There was one of those pauses, while I checked around to see if I had a solemn oath on me. I don't have very many of them to begin with, having wasted a lot in my youth, and it didn't look as if I'd brought one along today. But one gives it the Valiant Effort, doesn't one?

"Terribly sorry, old man," I said by way of an apology. "I don't really mean to be in the way, you know. It's just one of those things that happen. Like floods and hurricanes."

"I don't give a damn about floods and hurricanes," Steinberg snarled, becoming positively menacing. "All I care about is getting this case wrapped up, and I'm going to do it with or without you. Clear?"

"I say—"

"Shut up! Now let's see the passage."

Steinberg preceded me into the passage, and I confess to being tempted to shut him in the thing and let him find his own damn way out, but then I had a sort of premonition of what his mood would be like when he did emerge, and I thought better of the whole silly plan. I followed him in, with Marie right behind me.

"You go downstairs," I pointed out.

"You don't say."

Policemen don't like to have things pointed out.

We passed the three empty cabinets and came to the fourth. It, too, was empty.

"I say!" I said.

"This the one that has the forty Mud Dancers, all in a row?"

"But—"

"Perhaps they're behind a secret panel behind the secret cabinet in the secret passage?" His voice dripped a rather viscous variety of sarcasm.

"They were there. Right on those shelves, not fifteen minutes ago." I turned to Marie for support.

"It's true, Sergeant. I saw them, too. I don't know what can have happened to them."

Steinberg nodded. "All right, let's go back upstairs."

We went. I mean, it seemed the prudent thing to do. Back in the study, Steinberg pulled out his notebook and pencil. That, I thought, boded no good whatsoever.

"Now, let's see what we have," he said in that slow, deliberate police manner. "Mr. Brett."

"Call me John."

"For the moment Mr. Brett will suffice. Now, you say that fifteen minutes ago, when you called me, which is about twenty minutes ago, there were some forty Mud Dancers down there."

"That's right."

"And you, Miss Kellerman, verify this?"

"I do."

"And now they're all gone. Right?"

"All but this one," I said, picking up the little beastie.

"All but that one, yes. Now, how do you suppose it all happened? Do you suppose that while you two were in here calling me, a third party sort of sashayed through with a packing box and made off with the Mud Dancers?"

"Nonsense," I snorted, and, if I do say so myself, it was rather a good snort, "whoever it was obviously went through the garage."

"Possible," Steinberg allowed. "Possible. But how about this? One of you had that Mud Dancer all along and decided to trump up a story about forty more when you found the secret passage. After all, right now is not the best time to have a Mud Dancer, is it?"

"That doesn't make any sense at all," Marie put in.

"No?"

"Of course not. If I had a Mud Dancer right now that I thought might be embarrassing, I'd simply smash it."

Steinberg nodded. "Smash it."

"Why not?"

"Why not, indeed?" At which point he picked up the Mud Dancer we had found and brought its head down hard on the coffee table. It smashed.

"That's very good," I observed.

"Aha!" Steinberg said triumphantly. "It's hollow."

"I could have told you that," I said.

"You could?"

"Certainly. All you had to do was ask."

"Hmm. Well, what's done is done. Besides, if there are forty more, I'm sure we'll find them before we're through."

"And if there aren't, you've just destroyed the evidence."

He considered a moment. "It's a possibility, I concede. But on the other hand, what was it evidence of? It wasn't as if it was found. All the prints on it would have been mine, yours and Miss Kellerman's. And this room is where it was supposed to be in the first place. So I don't think I've done much. Except a favor for you."

"For me?" I said.

"Of course. There've been so many Mud Dancers in this thing that one less will only help things. If we come up with another, at least we can be sure it isn't a repeat appearance of this one."

The man had a point, though it looked to me as if he was mainly covering for himself. I mean, smashing the thing like that really was rather childish, and childishness is not one of the attributes we admire in our policemen. There are many others, equally unpleasant, that we do admire, but childishness is not in the group. Ignorance, rudeness and corruption are acceptable; childishness is simply not to be tolerated. So Steinberg had covered, but it did make sense. It was about the last thing that did make sense that day.

XII

Edie charged in around noon, with her lawyer in tow. He looked a little less than his usual chipper self, and I gathered Edie had not taken kindly to the proceedings down civic center way.

"Children!" she sang out. "Someone pour me a drink. My God, you have no *idea* how inconvenient it is to be suspected of murder. And messy! Ink! All over my fingers! And nothing but a rough paper towel to wash it off with. And the place they keep you. Ghastly, that's what it is. Simply ghastly. They popped me in a cell with all kinds of riffraff. I demanded another one, but it didn't do any good. And someone had scratched "The World Belongs to Karl Marx" all over everything. Can you imagine! And in Beverly Hills, no less. It's disgraceful!"

"Settle down, Edie, you're out now," Armand said in his most soothingly legal tones.

"Out! You bet I'm out. I'm out fifty thousand dollars, that's what."

"You get it back. All you have to do is show up for your trial."

Edie rolled her eyes. "Listen to the man. My trial. I don't *want* a trial. I think I'll cancel the whole damned thing and go to Bermuda. They can keep the fifty thousand."

Armand looked pained, as lawyers always do when threatened with the loss of a trial.

"Oh, Edie, I don't think that would be wise," he intoned.

Personlly, I hate intonations, so I thought I'd throw in my two cents' worth. Not much, compared to Edie's fifty big ones (as I believe they call them in some circles), but still, it was something. "Perhaps you could make a deal with them. You could offer to throw in another fifty thousand if they'll just forget about the whole thing. Hello, Armand."

"Hello, Brett. What are you doing here? Mixed up in this, too?"

"John was there when Harry got shot," Edie said, stating the fact rather succinctly.

"Why don't they try him, then?"

"I guess I didn't make myself clear. John was there, but he didn't do it. My car did. Or rather, someone in my car. And with my gun. And that boy, Marie's brother. What was his name?"

"Calvin," Marie said, a dark look coming into her eyes.

I took her hand, hoping to give her comfort. She got a cramp instead.

"Yes, Calvin. They shot him with my gun, too. Fortunately, not from my car, so I can probably wiggle out of that one. But what am I going to do about Harry?"

"Don't worry, we'll get you out of it all," Armand said, patting her as if she were some sort of beagle.

"Well, for the moment I suppose we'd better go to his funeral. It's always interesting to go to a funeral when the subject was murdered. All the friends stay away, and all the morbid strangers show up."

"Edie!"

"Oh, never mind, Armand. I'm upset. Why don't you run along, so I can get ready. See you at the mortuary." She more or less pushed Armand out the front door, shut it behind him, then turned to Marie and me. "Christ, what a bore. I think he's looking forward to the trial. Says he's never handled a murder before. I'll have to find someone else. Do you suppose Clarence Darrow is frightfully expensive?"

"He's dead," Marie said.

"My God, when do you suppose that happened? Well, I'll just have to get out the yellow pages, or something. Now, Marie, what have you got picked out for me to wear to the festivities this afternoon?"

"That black dress we got at Magnin's yesterday—"

"Forget it. I'm not wearing black. I ran into Polly Merritt just as I was getting sprung from the slammer, and she cut me dead. Seems they've all decided I did it. So I think I'll just do what Harry would have wanted me to do and put on a smart red dress with thousands of beads and maybe some sandals. John, does the top still go down on that awful little car of yours?"

I nodded, fearing the worst.

"Good. Go home and put on some sports clothes. You know, like tennis clothes, or something. And put the top down. You're taking me to the funeral in your car, and I'm going to tell everyone we're driving to Baja for the weekend immediately after Harry gets planted. That should keep them all talking for weeks."

"Edie . . ." I began.

"Don't interrupt. This is the way Harry would have wanted me to do it. Dance at my funeral, he always said. So, fine! I'll dance! All my friends know exactly how I felt about Harry, and no matter what I do at the funeral, they'll know I loved him. As for the rest of them, they'd love to believe there's going to be a scandal, so let's give them their money's worth."

Marie looked horrified at the whole idea. I have to admit, it all sounded rather amusing to me, but if Marie was going to be horrified, I thought it was to my best interest to string along with her. I popped my eyes out to match hers.

"Mrs. Wilson," she said, "you can't do that!"

"I can't? Watch me."

"But the police are sure to be there. What will they think?"

"What they've been thinking all along. That John and I have been boffing and are going to go right on doing it. If I've got the name, I might just as well have the game. Or at least seem to. Now, scoot along, John, so Marie and I can find something really *déclassé* for me to wear."

I scooted, on the theory that if I refused, Edie would only pop me into some of Harry's more outlandish clothes, and, if I had to wear outlandish clothes to a funeral, I figured they might as well be mine. Mine at least fit, and I like to think my taste in outlandish clothes is better than Harry's.

After due consideration, I finally settled for a pair of pants subtly striped in lavender and lime green, with a white fishnet top to show off my chest, what there is of it. We English don't have much in the way of chests, actually. I suppose it comes from breathing a steady diet of fog in our youth. Cramps things up, no doubt. At any rate, I got myself togged out and returned to the Wilson manse. Marie was not pleased.

"Oh, my God, John," she breathed upon seeing me. "You aren't going to wear that to the funeral?"

"Oh, rather. Don't you like it?"

"It's indescribable. It looks like Easter Parade on Fire Island."

"I thought you said it was indescribable," I said a bit sourly.

Then Edie appeared, and while the outfit wasn't red, it was resplendent. She had managed to find a peasant skirt in about fifteen nauseous spring colors, and she wore one of Harry's white shirts, the tails tied across her belly *à la South Pacific*. Her feet were clad in a pair of Joan Crawford wedgies, with ankle straps up to her knees, and she'd made good on the bead threat. It looked as if she'd bought out two entire branches of Woolworth's. She had her hair pulled back into a ponytail to complete the effect.

"Do you love it?" she asked.

"It's irresistible. All you need is a couple of flowers in your hair. Daisies, perhaps."

"Marvelous. We'll stop on the way and pick some up. Where did you get that terrible shirt?"

"I rather like it," I said, looking as offended as possible.

"On a lifeguard, fine. But don't you think you're a little . . . puny?"

I chose to overlook it. People have remarked on my puniness before, to no avail. I am still puny and intend to remain so. I've found it keeps me out of trouble. Despite the comic papers, people don't spend all their time kicking sand in my face, and I've noticed that it's usually the big fellows who get involved in fights. Those of us who know we would lose tend to avoid trouble. Let the endomorphs kill each other off, is my motto. We ectomorphs shall prevail in the end.

The three of us left, Edie and I in the Sunbeam, with Marie following along in Edie's Rolls. I stopped to pick up the required daisies, and Edie spent the rest of the trip to the mortuary twining them in her hair, giving herself a sort of jaded Mother Nature look. It was all rather disgusting.

Nothing much happened during the service. It was on the way to the cemetery that things started popping. To begin with, Edie refused the services of the limo, which I thought was wasteful, considering she had paid for it. Rather, she insisted I drive the Sunbeam directly behind the hearse, with her seated on the rear deck, tossing daisies to the passersby. At one point she ran out and stopped the whole procession while she went into a florist's to restock. I don't think Beverly Hills has seen anything quite like it in a long time.

By the time we reached the grave, a goodly part of the parade had given it up as a bad scene and gone home. Consequently, there were more than enough chairs to go around. Edie saw fit to stop the service during the first hymn and yoo-hoo to Steinberg, who had been trying to be inconspicuous at the rear. She insisted he take a seat next to her, thus lousing up his chance to see who was in attendance.

I, on the other hand, was shrewder. Or, more properly, a lot more brazen. Steinberg, of course, had his position to think about (the one with the Beverly Hills fuzz, not the one next to Edie), and that may have cramped what little style he had. I, however, was not so encumbered.

Taking my behavioral cue from the bereaved widow, who was by now wearing a rhinestone-studded black veil with a slash in it to allow for her cigarette holder, I merely stood on my chair during the eulogy and had a look around. What was left of the Beverly Hills gentry looked slightly aghast at this breach of etiquette, but most of them had been aghast that day to a degree which wore them out. By the time I was discovered standing on the chair, those who weren't already shell-shocked were busy snapping candid shots of the unique behavior of the widow and her party. At any rate, I stood on the chair, and nobody objected. The crowd, as I viewed it from my vantage point, was a playback of the last three days of my life.

Marie, of course, was beside me, but her uncle, the good James Hinman, was tucked in next to a tree about halfway back. In front of him sat Hans von Berlin with the ever-popular Elsa, and hiding with the rest of the Beverly Hills types were the Kauffmans, Mr. and Mrs.

All that remained to complete the picture was Harry Gotham. I sat down again and wondered to Marie why they had all showed up.

"Why who all showed up?" she said, giving evidence of having been paying attention to the services.

"All of them. Hans von Berlin. Your uncle. The Kauffmans."

"The Kauffmans? Are they here?"

"Back with the Beverly Hills crowd. Did they know old Harry?"

She shrugged. "Not that I know of. I want to see them. Which ones are they?"

"He's wearing a blue pinstriped double-breasted suit, and she has on the flowered print number. You'll have to stand on the chair," I instructed her.

Generally, Marie would not have been the type of girl to bounce up on her chair at a funeral. I want to make this clear, as I have a certain respect for Marie. She isn't at all like me. Decorous. That's the word for Marie. Definitely decorous. The situation, though, was not general, so I suppose Marie was able to suspend general behavior for the moment. I mean, precedents had been set that day, and the public, as it were (and what was left of it), was prepared. Consequently, Marie popped up on her chair to have a little look. I heard her gasp. Not a little gasp, but one of those jolly big ones that portend an impending heart failure. A dramatic gasp. I looked up as she sat down.

"My God," she breathed. She was as pale as a sheet.

"Did you see them?"

"Yes. But *he's* back there."

"Who?"

"Him. Gotham. Harry Gotham."

"You're kidding."

"John, he is! I saw him. Look for yourself."

Up I went again, for a quick resurveyal. Sure enough, the girl's assessment was borne out. There he was, Harry Gotham in the flesh (and the wig), tucked over behind a bush, or perhaps it was a fern, trying to be inconspicuous. In fact, it was the same bush Steinberg had been trying to look inconspicuous behind when Edie had blown his cover, as it were. Having made the identification, I sat down again.

I thought things over and decided it would be best to alert Steinberg. He had been showing a distinct aversion lately to being left out of my plans, and this seemed a good time to prove my good faith. Besides, he was right here, and it didn't seem likely that a frontal attack on Gotham would go unnoticed. I leaned across Edie to apprise him of the situation.

"Psst," I hissed.

"Shhhh!" Edie snapped, raising my eyebrows.

"I didn't know you were following the service," I said.

"I'm not," she said. "I'm listening to the financial news." She raised a corner of the veil to reveal a portable radio clamped to her ear.

"Swap places with me. I have to talk to Steinberg."

The switch was made with remarkably little fuss. I put my mouth to Steinberg's ear. "Psst!" I hissed again, not wanting to raise my voice.

"What the hell is it now, Brett?"

"Herbie," I said, reverting to the familiar, "Harry Gotham's standing back there."

"Sure he is," Steinberg replied. "And Greta Garbo is with him."

I gathered he didn't believe me.

"Really, old man," I insisted, "he is. Right by that bush you were behind before Edie called you."

"If you think I'm going to stand up on my chair and have a look, you can think again."

"All right. But let's grab him."

"Grab him?" Steinberg looked baffled.

"Certainly. I'll go around one way, and you go around the other, and we'll trap him in the bush."

Steinberg eyes rolled. "Brett, you *are* a winner. Nobody does those things. They're strictly Keystone Kops."

I drew myself up, wounded. Apparently subtlety was going to be required. Well, I can be as subtle as the next man. (Subtle, in fact, might have been my middle name, except that my mother had a very rich uncle whose rather unlikely name she slapped on me. Not that it did any good; when the old goat died, it was discovered that he had left his entire estate to three bastard sons born to him by a member of the fallen Bulgarian aristocracy. The Bulgarians always win.) I called my stores of subtlety to the front.

"Maybe that's why there's so many crooks on the loose," I said.

"What?" Steinberg apparently wasn't following. I guessed I had been too subtle.

"Well, you can't expect to catch them if you don't try, can you?" I sat back to let my words take effect. There was a long silence, interrupted only by the words of the minister, while Steinberg perked.

Finally, he nodded. "OK, Brett, we'll try it. But I warn you . . ." he trailed off, leaving the air thick with something.

We decided I would go back around Edie, in a more or less eastward direction, and Steinberg would head west, our paths thus not crossing. Then we would both turn north, dashing past the crowd of mourners. At the final moment, I would make a hard left turn and Herbie would make a hard right, putting the bush and Gotham between us. Then we would close in for the kill. It was decided that the signal for our mission to commence would be the minister uttering the words, "my cup runneth over," from the Twenty-third Psalm, at which point we would runneth over to the bush and comfort old Gotham with any rods and staffs that happened to be around.

Everything went according to plan, more or less. There were, of course, a few hitches, as there were likely to be with a delicate operation such as I have outlined above. For instance, it developed that the minister wasn't going to recite the Twenty-third Psalm, and I had to have Edie request it. Apparently, special requests from the audience aren't normal procedure at funerals; the minister seemed a bit upset. I guess it interrupted the flow of his act. Edie, however, threatened to stop payment on his gratuity check, so he plopped the old psalm into the show. At the cue, Herbie and I took off. This upset Edie, who apparently thought an air raid had begun. At any rate, no sooner had I dashed in front of her than she screamed and charged forward. This accomplished little except knocking old Harry, complete with casket, into the grave prematurely, with Edie and her radio following. Somehow the volume on the radio got knocked up, and the crowd was treated to the Dow-Jones averages emanating from Harry Wilson's grave. In retrospect, it seems appropriate.

I was, of course, unaware of those proceedings, as I was involved in the logistics of the capture. Keeping my head low and counting on my sense of direction and distance to guide me, I charged around the teeming mob and headed straight for the bush. Gotham had disappeared, but I had expected that. Faced with a charging John Brett, I'm sure that I, too, would take cover. He was, no doubt, cowering in the vegetation.

I dove in, and sighting a body, grabbed. A struggle ensued, with the two of us alternately gaining the advantage. First he was on top, then I. Then he, then I. I wondered what was holding Herbie up and finally yelled for him. I mean, I wasn't getting the best of things, and it seemed to me only fair that Herbie should help.

To make a long story short, it quickly developed that the body I had grabbed was Herbie, not Gotham. The struggle stopped, and we lay there in the bush, panting. Gotham had disappeared. Not a trace. Most vexing.

It was then that we noticed a slight itching on our hands and faces. It seems the bush that Gotham had been next to was one of those obnoxious plants known as nettles. Most distressing. Most distressing, indeed.

XIII

I was, I regret to say, incommunicado for the next day. Nettles have that effect on me—they tend to make my face swell up to rather remarkable proportions and give me an adolescent look that can only be described as less than attractive. A lot less than attractive. And since my hands matched my face, and the whole thing was less than comfortable, I was housebound. I received a call from Herbie Steinberg, and he, too, was housebound, which was just as well for me, as he gave me a vivid description of what he would do to me if he could get his hands on me. I pointed out that, in the condition his hands were in, the proposed plan of action would doubtless be as painful for him as for me, but he wasn't impressed.

Marie showed up around noon, loaded down with soothing balms and poisonous-looking lotions, and proceeded to lather me up with one thing and another. I can't say the treatment did anything spectacular for the nettles, but my ego got a good boost out of it all. By the time she was finished, West

Ninth Street was blessed with a swollen and itching Englishman who reeked of jungle gardenia. Not pleasant, either to the eye or the nose, but Marie bore up admirably.

Nettles, I have come to believe, have strange powers on the thought processes. It might perhaps be a good idea for a team of scientists and/or psychologists to obtain some sort of government grant for a study of this subject. I mean, if grants can be given out for studies of the effects of grass on the brain, why not nettles? There isn't that much difference, is there?

Be that as it may, those nettles made me think. Or at least gave me time to think, for I won't say one's life comes to a dead halt when one is down with nettles, but one doesn't trot off to the smarter watering holes when one has nettles, does one? (No, if anyone is interested, one does not.) So there I was for many hours, just me and my nettles, and an occasional spot of tea with perhaps just a hint of bourbon for flavor. So I thought about things.

There had been something about the funeral that had bothered me. I couldn't quite put my finger on it (if minds have fingers), but it seemed to me there was something I had seen and then hadn't seen. I kept grasping at it, and it kept slipping away. Frustrating, that's what it was. Then I decided to go over the whole business once more, from beginning to end, and see if I could put the pieces together. After all, if Hercule Poirot and all that crowd can figure things out with brain power alone, there isn't any reason why John Brett can't.

Doing things systematically, I began at the beginning and proceeded toward the nettle bush; then I began at the nettle bush and went backwards. On both occasions, I found myself sticking on the place where I stood up at the funeral to have a look at Gotham. My mind, like a zoom lens, focused on the incident. Then I had it. The first time I stood up, I saw Hans von Berlin, but not Gotham. The second time, I saw Gotham, *but not Hans von Berlin*. Significant, I thought, very significant.

I will modestly confess that I was rather proud of myself. It was the same feeling I used to get when, as a small child, I would complete the edge of a jigsaw puzzle: a quiet pride in accomplishment. (Honesty compels me to admit that, as a small child, I never finished *more* than the edge of a jigsaw puzzle, but for me, the quiet pride of accomplishment in completing the edge was enough. I was that kind of small child. Perhaps that's why people were always kicking me.)

For me, it was but a short leap in the logical process to figure out that von Berlin and Gotham were one and the same person. I mean, if first one is there, and then the other is there, but they're not there at the same time, it stands to reason that they're the same person, doesn't it? Of course it does.

Then, working on the assumption that von Berlin and Gotham were one and the same, I fitted this new person (or persons) into the general scheme of things. I will concede that it was a tight fit. I mean, after I'd programmed von Berlin/Gotham in, I came up with a rather startling question: So what? The only thing it solved was the reason why no one had been able to locate Harry Gotham. But it was a beginning.

I apprised Marie of my startling discovery and suggested we call Steinberg immediately. She thought it over and expressed doubts that he would be impressed but conceded we might as well give it a whirl. I didn't feel like coping with the telephone in my weakened condition, so Marie made the connection for me. The conversation follows:

"Is that you, Herbie?"

"Oh, my God." (In a hopeless tone of voice, which I considered most uncalled-for.)

"I know where Gotham is."

"Good for you. In another nettle bush?"

"No. He's Hans von Berlin."

"He's who?"

"Hans von Berlin."

"How nice for him." (Steinberg hung up. Very rude, if you ask me.)

"You were right," I told Marie. "He hung up."

She nodded. "Well, you have to admit, it isn't much. I mean, von Berlin could have just walked away, you know."

"Of course, he could have. But he didn't. It was all done with masks."

"Oh, John. You've seen Gotham close up. Did his face look like a mask?"

Well, as a matter of fact it did and not a very good one, but that wasn't what she meant.

"Well, no, but he could have been using makeup. I'm sure a good disguise artist could do the job. It's just a matter of adding some wrinkles and that terrible wig. The clothes would have to change. Gotham always dressed forty years younger than he was."

She nodded again, apparently pondering the thing out in her own mind. Then she seemed to come to a decision, and her whole being brightened. It almost made me forget about the nettles.

"And von Berlin recommended Gotham to the Wilsons, didn't he?"

"That's what they tell me. Now suppose, just suppose, that Harry Wilson and von Berlin were in the dope thing together. They invent Harry Gotham to get in and out of the Wilsons' house as a courier."

Marie shook her head. "But Gotham's been around for a long time, and he was only at the Wilsons' once."

I considered it. Suddenly everything wasn't as neat as I had thought. Then I remembered Lompoc.

"Let's go to Lompoc. We'll call von Berlin's showroom, and if he's there, and my theory's right, the place in Lompoc should be deserted, and we can have a look around."

"And if he's not there?"

"Then we wait till tomorrow, or whenever we find him at his office."

Marie didn't seem terribly enthusiastic about the idea, but she agreed that it was probably worth a try. I didn't know what I expected to find in Lompoc, but I was bound and determined to go. It proved, eventually, to be an error. Well, those things happen.

After dousing me down again with all the condiments, Marie left to go to her brother's funeral. I had intended to accompany her, but, what with my

appearance and all, it didn't seem to be in order.
Instead I made another pot of tea and called Edie.

"How are you, darling?" she cried when I identified myself.

"Barely surviving. How about you?"

"I'm afraid I twisted my knee when I followed
Harry into the grave. Other than that, fine. Have you
figured out who shot Harry yet? I'll bet it was that
awful Gotham."

"It wasn't Gotham. He doesn't exist."

"He doesn't? But I met the man. I'll admit I didn't
like him, but he was definitely here."

"No, he wasn't. But that isn't the point. Edie, old
thing—"

"Don't call me old!"

"Sorry. Anyway, would you mind coming over?"

"Wouldn't I be in the way?"

"The way? Oh. Oh, no, Marie went to her
brother's funeral. Anyway, I want to talk to you."

"Talk. I'm here."

"Well, um, there might be, you know . . . bugs."

"Oh. Yes. Well, stir up some martinis, and I'll be
right along."

I muddled with the gin and vermouth, and Edie
arrived in short order, her knee smartly bandaged in
black satin. She made herself at home and promptly
flushed down a drink. I refilled her, then we got
down to business. I filled her in on the secret passage and what I had found there. Then I asked her
what she thought about the possible relationship between Harry and drugs.

"I mean," I said, putting it as delicately as possible, "that if Harry was dealing in liquor when that

was illegal, mightn't he have been dealing in drugs now, for fun rather than profit?"

Edie considered it for a moment. "I suppose it's possible. I don't know. He was always up to something to stem the boredom. But drugs seem a bit far out, even for Harry. Harry believed in booze. He used it himself and didn't see why other people shouldn't. But drugs can hurt people, and I just don't think Harry would have had anything to do with something like that."

"But there's the secret passage," I pointed out.

"So? Obviously, someone other than Harry knew about it, if all that stuff got taken out after he was killed. Maybe Harry himself didn't know about it.

"Oh, come now."

Edie poured herself another drink. "No, really, John. If the secret passage was there ever since the house was built, Harry might not have known about it. And Philippine mahogany doesn't sound like anything very new."

"OK, we'll assume Harry didn't know about the passage. Who did?"

"Who knows?"

"Who was the last owner of the house?"

"Harry's company. They still own it. It was a foreclosure years ago, during the Depression. When I saw it, it was empty, and I liked it, so Harry leased it from the company."

"But you don't know who owned it first?"

"Of course not. But you could find out easily enough. Look it up in the Hall of Records."

That seemed a good idea, so I filed it away in my mind under Things to Do Tomorrow, and Edie and I got down to some serious drinking. Nettles may do wonderful things for the mind, but liquor does wonderful things for nettles. By the time Marie got back from the funeral, I'm afraid Edie and I were pretty well shot. I stood up, more or less, when Marie came in.

"Good funeral?" I inquired.

"You're drunk," she said accusingly.

"Rather. Yes. Rather."

"Oh, sit down, Marie. The poor dear's all full of thorns, and I've wrecked my knee and become a widow and murder suspect, and John's got the cops mad at him, too, so we're celebrating. Have a drink."

"I can't."

"Of course you can," I said. "I'll put one in a glass for you."

"No, I can't, really. The funeral was too depressing, and if I have a drink, I'll start crying and be all messy."

"Oh, now, that's all right," Edie said in her most comforting, if slurred, tones. "A little cry never hurt anyone."

"Well, I don't want to cry. I just want to find out who killed Calvin."

"Whoever killed Harry killed Calvin," Edie said, beginning to sway a little.

"And whoever killed Calvin killed Harry," I put in helpfully.

Marie finally broke down.

"But who killed them?" she screamed, bursting into tears.

The damage now being done, I poured her a drink which she quickly drained, and I poured her another. She sat sobbing quietly for a while, and I put a rather bloated arm around her. I don't know whether it was the gin, my arm or the jungle gardenia, but eventually she quieted down, and the sobbing stopped.

"That's much better," Edie said. "A good cry always clears the mind. Harry always used to tell me that. I think I'd better go along now. I really don't think you two need me."

"But Mrs. Wilson," Marie said, pulling herself together, "do you think you can drive?"

"Don't worry about a thing. All I'm going to do is crawl around the corner to Secret Harbor and take up residence in the bar. They can shovel me out whenever they feel so moved."

She weaved out and somehow managed to make it to her car. I lost track after that as Marie had nestled herself in my arms, putting me into the Big Strong Man role, a role I seldom play. However, I rose to the occasion with the help of the gin and the bourbon. Strength In Booze, as the saying goes. The effect, though, was somewhat diminished by my nettled appearance. What I mean is, it isn't easy to play the Big Strong Man when you're swollen, smashed, itching and reeking of jungle gardenia. The whole effect is rather more on the lines of a refugee from a hairdressers' Sunday picnic molested by a batch of enraged hornets. On the other hand, it was the best I could do under the circumstances.

Marie seemed to appreciate my effort, if not my results, and we sat cuddling and guzzling for a while. Eventually, one or the other of us, I don't really remember which, fixed some dinner, then we got back to the more serious business. Namely, the cuddling and the guzzling.

Somewhere around midnight, the good old hour of sin, Marie drew herself up. "John," she said, looking me straight in the eye, "who killed them?"

I returned her look, feeling terribly stalwart. "I don't know," I said, "but I mean to find out."

With that, we went to bed, with every intention of indulging in some of the sin it was the hour of. Unfortunately, in the middle of our sinning, we both passed out.

XIV

The morning was somewhat fogged over, but with the help of some revoltingly strong coffee, I was able to pull the personal self more or less together. Dispatching Marie to tend to Edie's business for a while, I betook myself to what is euphemistically known as the Hall of Records.

I say euphemistically because it strikes me that the more honest name for said institution might be Bureau of Theft Registry. After all, the whole theory of the outfit is that there should be records to prove who owns what. But it's rather like a batch of thieves sitting around, proving to each other that the car Paul stole from George is truly Paul's simply because Paul is stronger than George, or Paul speaks English while George is stuck with some primitive language like Piute or Spanish. I mean, let's face it. The whole legitimacy of a land title is based on who stole what from whom during the most recent social upheaval. Be that as it may, there I was, prepared to engage the Bureaucracy in its lair. It isn't one of my favorite pastimes, but sometimes it becomes necessary.

I picked out a particularly innocuous-appearing old man for my initial skirmish. He seemed to have been around the place for some three or four centuries, and I thought he would undoubtedly have the location of all pertinent documents on the tip of his tongue. Perhaps he did. The only question was whether or not he had a tongue.

I adopted one of my superior looks in an attempt to pass myself off as a high-level type, perhaps a new appointee checking the lay of the land. It quickly developed that he was used to dealing with politically powerful incompetents.

"The records for Beverly Hills, please," I snapped, resisting an impulse to slap the desk with a swagger stick. (The fact that I wasn't carrying a swagger stick may have helped me resist the above impulse. I don't know.) He didn't even look up.

"Zone?" he muttered.

"Pardon?" I retorted, letting him know I wasn't used to having my demands left unmet.

"Zone," he repeated.

"What zone?"

"How would I know?" he asked, beginning to look annoyed. "You're the one who wants to know who owns something, not me."

I began to get annoyed. It seemed I had run into a veteran. "I mean, what zone information do you need?"

"Zip code. Doing everything by zip code now. Makes it easier, except that no one knows what the zip codes are except the post office." This seemed to amuse him, and he gave out with a sort of chuckle. An unpleasant sort.

My computerlike mind remembered seeing a zip code map in an old phone book once, and it struck me that a public building was not likely to have current phone books. Perhaps I had found a way out.

"Got a phone book?" I asked, trying not to sound suspicious.

He was on to that one, and another chuckle gurgled forth.

"Phone booths are in the basement," he said.

"I don't want a booth, just a book."

"Got a requisition?"

Obviously, it was going to be one of those days. Whipped, I oozed out to find the phone booths. I have no doubt in my mind whatever that that dirty old man got on the phone instantly and called ahead. When I got to the basement, I found nothing but brand-new phone books, unmarked, untorn, uncreased, with not a zip code map in the lot. I moved on to the information desk, where a cute blonde of about sixty-five was perched, vulturelike, waiting for victims.

"May I help you?" she sneered, obviously hoping to be able to lead me astray.

"I hope so. What's the zip code for Beverly Hills?"

"The post office is two blocks west, sir," she said, grinning wickedly.

"I don't care where the post office is. All I want is the zip code for Beverly Hills."

"Postal information must be obtained from that agency, sir. This is information for the Hall of Records." She turned away, and so did I.

It occurred to me that perhaps I might do better to call the post office than to hike over there, so I retreated once more to the basement. After being transferred three times and cut off twice, I was given zip code information. I asked once more for the Beverly Hills digits. The man on the other end was most gracious.

"That information is listed in your zip code directory," he informed me.

"But I don't *have* a zip code directory!" I screeched. I don't normally like to screech, but sometimes it's necessary.

"You may order one by writing to the post office nearest you."

An idea struck. "That would be Beverly Hills," I purred.

"Fine," he said. "Just address your request to Postmaster, Beverly Hills, California, nine oh two one two."

"*Sucker!*" I screamed, slamming the phone down and dancing across the corridor. My first victory of the day. I dashed back up the stairs, foregoing the elevator, and found the old man again.

"Nine two oh one two!" I bellowed. He looked at me questioningly, as if a retarded pigeon had just stumbled in.

"That's the zip code I want. Beverly Hills. Nine two oh one two."

He shook his head. "Beverly Hills is nine oh two one two."

There was a long silence while I sized him up. It became clear that the man was far too old for me to attack. Finally I spoke. "You mean you knew all along?"

He beamed. "I know every zip code in the country. Used to work for the post office."

"Why didn't you say so?"

"You didn't ask. All you wanted to know was where you could find a phone book."

I decided on the spot that if I ever become a citizen of this country, I shall vote no on all raises for public employees.

To make a long story short, the rest of the morning was spent in the same sort of dickering, I trying to get information, he trying to conceal it. I've noticed that over the years, public employees, dealing with public funds and public information, always take it upon themselves to regard the public's property as their own, not to be given out to just any old citizen who happens around. Let alone any old resident alien. However, after lots of jockeying, and tracing down of lot numbers and tract numbers and plat maps, and other boring things, the truth finally came out. I got a look at the records on Edie's house.

There they all were. Deeds and mortgages and policies of title insurance and quitclaims, right back to the original thefts, which had been made first by a Spaniard, then by a Mexican, then by an American. Perhaps the Chinese will be next.

At any rate, it was the work of only an hour to trace the ownership from Harry Wilson's bank back to the previous owner. All the records were there, of course, but I'm not very good at sorting out mortgages and foreclosures, and all that. For a long time, it appeared that Transamerica Title and Trust Insurance Company owned everything lock, stock and barbed wire. But it turned out not to be true. Not true at all.

I made copies of the pertinent deed, mortgage and foreclosure, thanked the old buzzard who had been so helpful and was on my way. I wondered, as I headed for Edie's house, just what I was going to tell Marie. I mean, my pet theory seemed to be knocked into the traditional cocked hat. The previous owner, it seems, had been one Harry Gotham. Rats.

Marie, for her part, was less than sympathetic. "Well, you have to admit, John," she said, "it really was a silly idea."

"Not silly at all," I said, feeling a bit sulky. "It was just the kind of thing that would have made sense. I had it all so neatly tied up, except for how Harry got killed. And I'll bet I could have fitted that in, too."

"If you ask me, it's neater with Harry Gotham around. He could have done it all easily. He knew the whole house, and he could have gotten in and out of the passage through the garage. For all we know, he might have been in the passage all the time you and Steinberg were here after Harry got shot. He could have driven Edie's car back and hidden in the passage."

"Nonsense," I said, sounding as pompous as possible. "The cops were all around the place. He couldn't have gotten out again. Besides, how did he get Edie's keys?"

"Simple," Marie said, looking smug. "All he had to do was come in through the passage and pick

them out of her purse. The gun was in the car, so
that wasn't any problem. Then he drops the car
back, takes the gun and the Mud Dancer, and goes
home."

"And shoots Calvin?" It all seemed a bit unlikely.

"Well, why not?"

"Why not? Why? You have to have a motive."

Marie thought a while, and I could see the little
cells spinning about in her head. "OK," she said finally. "Try this. Mr. Wilson somehow found the passage and figured out what was going on. Gotham felt
threatened, because Mr. Wilson was going to turn
him over to the law. So Gotham shot Harry. Maybe
he shot Calvin for the same reason."

"Calvin was a junkie," I pointed out. "It isn't
likely a junkie is going to turn in his connection."

"But Gotham wasn't a connection anymore.
Maybe Calvin needed a fix, and Gotham had to tell
him the whole system was shot, that Mr. Wilson had
found the stash. So if Gotham can't supply him anymore, Calvin wouldn't have any reason to shield
him. So Gotham shoots Calvin."

It all sounded logical. There didn't seem to be any
reason why Gotham *couldn't* have been running a
dope ring out of his former residence. On the other
hand, there didn't seem to be much reason why he
would be. I mean, if I were going to run a dope ring,
I don't think I'd choose to house it in a place I'd
been kicked out of a couple of decades before. I decided that a trip to Lompoc was definitely in order. I
was in the process of planning it with Marie when
Edie arrived.

"Have you got me off the hook yet, John?" She seemed rather flip about the whole thing, if you ask me.

"No. Harry doesn't seem to be involved, though. It's Marie's theory that it was Gotham's show all the way through."

We briefed her on the Gotham theory, and she, who really should have been interested in proving he did it all, pointed out another hole.

"If he was up to no good in my basement, it was rather silly of him to come waltzing around here as a decorator, wasn't it?"

I declined to answer, figuring Marie could defend her own damn theory. I liked mine involving Hans von Berlin much better, anyway. Even more if I could fit that repulsive Nazi receptionist of his into it. As for Marie, she seemed a bit stumped.

"How do I know why he came around as a decorator? Maybe he was afraid the redecorating would uncover the secret passage."

"Jesus!" said Edie. "All I was going to do was change the drapes, not rip out the damn walls.

"He didn't know that." Stubborn girl, Marie. "Besides, it could have been coincidence. If Hans von Berlin told him about the job, what could he say? 'Sorry, but I'm running dope through there'? Not likely."

"All right," Edie replied. "Let's assume Gotham did it. Better he than I. Where is he?"

"That," I said, "is the question of the day. He has a place up at Lompoc, wherever that is, and Marie and I were planning a little jaunt up there."

"Fine. I'll just go along. We can pack a picnic and take the Rolls. When do we leave?"

I pointed out that the whole thing wasn't just a ride in the country, and that Gotham (if there was a Gotham) was a rather dangerous sort, and that I didn't think charging into Lompoc in a gold Rolls-Royce would be exactly subtle. But Edie was determined.

"Ridiculous," she snapped. "I'm not afraid of a silly decorator with a wig, and, besides, I'm the prime suspect in the case. I think I have a right to be in on things."

As a sort of last-ditch effort, I mentioned to her that Steinberg would undoubtedly be displeased if she began making unauthorized trips into the hinterlands. She passed that off as being a restriction applicable only to petty criminal types: certainly, it didn't apply to her; she was, after all, a respected pillar of the community. Apparently, she didn't regard being a murder suspect as being detrimental to the reputation. Come to think of it, I can't really see why it should be. I'm sure lots of the best people have done in an uncle or two in their time. Certainly, such things never bothered the old royalty back on the native soil.

Nonetheless, I decided that Steinberg should be apprised of the upcoming expedition, so I stopped by the old HQ to brighten up his day.

I regret to have to report that his nettles hadn't cleared up as quickly as my own. Perhaps if he had been blessed with Marie's tender ministrations . . .

but, of course, if he had been, I wouldn't have been, and, well . . . yes. Tough about his nettles.

I don't think he was pleased to see me. I'm almost sure he uttered a rather unpleasant word when I presented myself. Suggested an unnatural relationship with my mother, if I interpreted him correctly. Disgusting idea.

We got down to the issues of the day almost instantly, what with my refusing to discuss the events at old Harry's funeral. As far as I'm concerned, the past is the past and not to be brought up again, particularly when the past contains memorable moments such as that funeral. I brought him up to date on my activities, and he seemed impressed, for a change.

"And the Hall of Records is still there?" he said.

"Of course," I replied, as frostily as possible. I didn't approve of his implications. Didn't approve of them at all.

"So Harry Gotham used to own the Wilson place, did he?" Steinberg mused. "Very interesting. Very interesting."

"Isn't it?" I agreed, glad he'd finally found something interesting instead of lecturing me. I can stand only so much lecturing.

"Yes. Suppose Mrs. Wilson's lying about not having known who owned the place previously. Suppose she and Gotham have known each other for years. Known each other very well. It thickens the soup, doesn't it?"

I looked at him accusingly, whatever that means. "Sir," I said, drawing myself up to my full height and beetling my brows, "you have a dirty mind!"

Steinberg nodded. "True. This business tends to develop one. Anyway, it's an interesting possibility. Where do you suppose Gotham is?"

"Edie and Marie and I thought we'd have a drive up to Lompoc tomorrow and see if he's there."

"Lompoc?" Steinberg seemed lost.

Then I remembered. I'd been concealing evidence again. I must learn not to do that. "Oh, didn't I tell you? Gotham has a country place up there." I passed it off as smooth as you please. There was a long pause, while Steinberg's blood pressure climbed. I could see he was having trouble containing himself.

"No, Brett," he said finally, forcing each word out from his somewhat clenched teeth, "you didn't tell me."

"Sorry about that, old chap. Must have slipped my mind. Anyway, we thought we'd just drive up there tomorrow and case the place."

"Case." The teeth were still clenched, though loosening a bit.

"Isn't that the right word?"

"It'll do until something better comes along. Of course, Mrs. Wilson is aware she isn't supposed to leave town?"

"She doesn't feel such rules apply to her."

"She wouldn't. Well, I won't try to stop you—it wouldn't be worth the possible consequences. The nettles are bad enough. God knows what you could do if you put your mind to it."

I had a sudden thought. "Why don't you come along?" I suggested.

He looked at me with the expression of a man who's just heard his death sentence pronounced.

"Not a chance," he said. "I already have a medal for performance above and beyond the call of duty. I don't have to go to Lompoc with you three." Then he brightened. "Hey! Maybe Gotham will catch you up there and knock you *all* off. Lompoc isn't in my jurisdiction!"

The man positively gloated. Rude, I call it. Very rude.

XV

Expedition Day began with one of those early-morning phone calls that I'm not particularly well equipped to deal with. For me, finding the phone in the morning is ordinarily a thirty-minute ordeal. I don't think my phone likes me any more than I like it, and I'm convinced it spends the dark hours before dawn creeping about the place, nestling into unlikely corners. That particular morning, it was discovered behind the toilet. I'm told that armadillos are fond of sleeping around toilets. I was unaware that telephones had the same rather unhealthy desires.

At the other end of the line was the respected Steinberg. I regarded it as an ill omen.

"Brett?" he snarled.

"I suppose so," I replied. The final verification had not yet been made.

"I'm going with you."

"Where?"

"Lompoc. Or has the trip been canceled?" He sounded hopeful.

"Oh. No. I guess I'd better get ready."

"Can you pick me up?"

"You're really going?" I asked, a bit incredulously.

"I have to. I mentioned what you were up to, to the chief, and he told me I had to go along."

"How sporting of him."

"That's not what I called it," he growled.

"Oh? What did you call it?"

"It's illegal to use profanity over the telephone, Brett."

"It's illegal to enter without a warrant, too."

"Shut up, Brett. Besides, you opened the door, not me."

"Merely a matter of priority. You were there."

"Anyway, can you pick me up?"

"What time?"

"I don't care. What time are you leaving?"

"Whenever I get ready. I haven't even gotten dressed yet. I'm curled up naked on my bathroom floor. How long do you think it will take me to uncurl?"

"Brett, you're impossible. Just swing by on your way to the Wilsons'. I'll be waiting." He hung up without saying good-bye, a habit of his I shall never get used to. It seems so abrupt, if you know what I mean.

I uncurled and pulled myself together. I had some old safari clothes left over from better days and soon got myself decked out in khaki shorts, an Eisenhower jacket and pith helmet. All that was left was to don my tennis shoes (which had turned pink

when I accidentally washed them with a red sweat-
shirt one day), and I was ready.

As instructed, I went first to the Beverly Hills Police Department. I left the Sunbeam in front and
walked up to the desk, where a rather goggle-eyed
fellow gave me the once-over. I asked for Steinberg.
Without taking his eyes off me, he picked up a
phone.

"Herb? Eddie here. There's a fellow out here
looking for you. He's wearing shorts, a combat
jacket and pink sneakers. Want me to bust him? No?
You're kidding!" He hung up. "Sit down, buddy.
He'll be right out."

In a minute, Steinberg came through. I say came
through because he didn't stop, or speak, or even
slow down. Just sort of waggled a finger at me. I
trotted after him and got to the Sunbeam only a pace
or two behind. He jumped in and sat staring straight
ahead.

"Hello," I said, trying to be friendly.

"Just get in, and let's get out of here," he snarled.

I complied, it seeming the best thing to do. We
rode in silence for a few blocks, then he seemed to
relax. Or at least the tension drained out of him, for I
heard a long sigh.

"John?" he said, sounding almost plaintive.

"Hmm?"

"John, did you *have* to wear pink tennis shoes?"

I didn't see why pink tennis shoes should bother
him. He must have seen a lot stranger things than
that in his time.

Marie opened the door for us at the Wilsons', and a slightly horrified look crossed her face. I guess she hadn't expected Steinberg. She recovered herself and let us in. "We're almost ready. Mrs. Wilson's upstairs dressing. Or aren't you going to let us go?" she said, challenging Steinberg with a look.

"Oh, no. Nothing like that. I'm going along. Chief's orders." Apparently, he wanted it made clear to everyone that he wasn't with us voluntarily.

Edie joined us in a few minutes, rather smartly togged out in a three-hundred-dollar peasant skirt from Magnin's, with her hair caught up by an emerald- and ruby-studded comb to match the colors of the skirt. Between the skirt and the comb was one of those see-through blouses. It would have helped if Edie still had had something to see, but that hadn't seemed to bother her. The blouse was mostly covered by a few hundred strings of beads, anyway. She had on a pair of flamenco shoes that, though they looked sturdy, boasted four-inch heels.

"Don't you love it?" she yelled. "I feel so *ethnic*!" Then she saw Steinberg. "John, I'm sure I've told you before not to bring dogs into the house."

"He's coming with us," I said.

"You're kidding. I'll feel like Jean Valjean traipsing arm in arm through the sewers with Javert."

I wasn't exactly sure what she meant. I suppose it was a reference to something ethnic.

Edie had had a picnic sent in by the Beverly Hills Hotel, and in a trice (or possibly two—I'm not sure how long a trice is), we were on our way.

I was driving, with Marie beside me; Edie and Steinberg sat in the back, getting acquainted. Edie was doing most of the talking, and every time I glanced in the mirror, Steinberg seemed to be sunk a little lower in his seat. He didn't speak at all for a long time; but finally, after about thirty minutes or so, a sound came out of him.

"Christ," he said. "Brett, where are we going?"

"Lompoc," I replied.

"Taking the scenic route?"

"Beg pardon?"

"This is the road to Bakersfield," he said, sounding pleased with himself.

Well, I admit that I made a mistake in navigation, but I don't really think it was my fault. I mean, all I'd been told was that Lompoc was north, and in Los Angeles, practically every damn road goes north. I corrected the error, and we floundered around in some place called Van Nuys for a while. It looks remarkably like Culver City and isn't any easier to get out of.

"Let's have a drink," Edie suggested, once we were back on the freeway.

Steinberg looked horrified. "It isn't legal to drink in a moving car," he said, sounding terribly policemanish.

"Don't be silly," Edie snapped. "If it weren't legal, they wouldn't put bars in these things."

With that she proceeded to whip up a shakerful of martinis. She offered me one, but I, in the interests of putting Herbie at ease, declined.

"No, thanks. Never drink while I drive. Only before."

Apparently, Steinberg decided to join them rather than try to beat them, for the next time I looked, he had a glass in his fist and was sipping merrily. There's something healthy about seeing an on-duty cop guzzling martinis in the back seat of a Rolls-Royce at ten o'clock in the morning. Something very healthy.

I wondered if his chief would have agreed with me.

Lompoc is one of those depressingly American towns with no middle and no edges. Somehow, the thing just sort of got started and grew. If it were European, it would at least have a semblance of form. A castle looming on a nearby hillside, perhaps, or some fortifications to protect it from invading Huns or Cossacks, or what-have-you. But no, Lompoc is American, with no starts or stops or centers of interest. As you drive in, there is a sort of main street, but you can't tell when you get to town, except for a sign that makes noble mutterings about churches with unlikely names like Kiwanis and Rotary.

Edie warned me as we approached. "John," she said, working on her fourth martini. "I don't want you to be disappointed, but Lompoc doesn't have a cathedral." With that, she settled back to gnaw on her olive.

All we were armed with, of course, was a post office box number, but I was counting on the local bureaucrats to be helpful. I thought Steinberg and his badge might also lend a little aid, but he had other ideas.

"Not a chance," he said when I broached the subject. "Not my territory at all. Besides, I've declared myself an observer only. Protecting my suspect, you might say. Gimme another martini, Edie. S'all right if I call you Edie?"

"You call me anything you want, dear. Just don't convict me," said Edie, pouring.

"I'll convict you of making the best damn martini this side of wherever we are."

I left them to their happy tippling and approached the post office. It turned out to boast one rather friendly looking woman standing behind a stamp sign. She was happily going through the FBI wanted posters when I got to the counter, looking, no doubt, for friends and relatives. Small towns are like that: a local criminal lends glamour to their otherwise squalid lives.

"I say," I began.

She looked up and smiled. "Limey, huh? Ain't seen one of you in a coon's age."

"Indeed?"

"Don't get much foreign trash around here. Lompoc's a nice town. What can I do for you?"

"I'm hoping for information.

"That's what they're all hoping for. Some of them get it; some of them don't." She almost destroyed herself with laughter. Her apparent thigh-slapper left me, shall we say, cold.

"I wonder if you can tell me who owns a particular post office box."

Her eyes narrowed. "That's confidential information. Can't give that out to nobody but the FBI." She thumped the posters appreciatively. "What's the number?"

"Seven forty-two," I said.

"Oh, yeah. That's the old queer with the wig. Harry Gotham's his name. Not local, so I guess it's all right if I tell you. He has a place out of town. If you ask me, he does bad things out there."

"Bad things?" I prompted her.

"Oh, you know. Naked swimming parties. Drinking. Things like that."

I nodded knowingly and tried to look prim. It isn't easy. "Is he there now?"

"I wouldn't know," she said, drawing her dignity around her like a faded housecoat. "It isn't my place to keep track of box holders. But he hasn't been around here lately."

I got instructions on how to get to Gotham's place and returned to the car. The only one left with a semblance of sobriety was Marie.

"Dd you find out anything?" she asked.

"The location of the house. They don't seem to like Gotham much in these parts, either. Not a very popular sort, is he?"

"I hope not. I want to see him gassed."

I didn't give her any answer, as I couldn't really think of one. I mean, what does one say to a comment like that? Instead, I started the car and headed out of town, or at least into the less populated regions.

We found Gotham's house on top of a hill. It was one of those ugly A-frame structures that seem to mess up more and more of the landscape. There wasn't any swimming pool in evidence, so I wondered where the naked swim-ins were taking place. Not that I really cared, of course, but the inquiring mind does wonder about such things, doesn't it?

We all piled out and approached the house. Taking the situation in hand, I knocked. Nothing happened.

"Maybe nobody's home," Steinberg said. "If not, let's go back to the car and have another martini."

"If not, let's break in," said Edie.

"That's illegal," said Steinberg.

"So is drinking on duty," said Edie.

I knocked again.

It soon became obvious that nobody was home, so I decided to act on Edie's suggestion, since Steinberg's really didn't seem to have much constructive potential. I smashed a window.

"Wanton destructiveness," muttered Steinberg.

We all trooped in and began inspecting the premises. Steinberg immediately discovered the bar, which wasn't remarkable when you consider that it occupied most of one wall.

"A bar," he squawked, descending upon it. I began to suspect that the good minion of the law was a secret alcoholic. "Edie, let's mix martinis."

They did.

Marie and I continued looking around, poking into this and that. Eventually, I discovered a chest that seemed shallower than it should have been. I called Steinberg over, and together we succeeded in clawing up a false bottom. Below it were what appeared to be the bottles from the secret passage.

"I says," I said. "These appear to be the bottles from the secret passage."

The ladies flocked round.

"I," Steinberg announced, "shall taste the contents of one of these bottles, determining for the benefit of all and sundry the contents."

With that he grabbed a bottle, pulled off the top and tasted it.

"Drugs," he said. "Definitely drugs." Then he passed out.

Edie and Marie and I continued upstairs, and at the back of one of the closets we found a boxful of Mud Dancers. That, we decided, was all we needed. We loaded the drugs, the Mud Dancers and Steinberg into the Rolls and adjourned. Then we thought better of it and returned a few of the bottles and a few of the Mud Dancers to the house, carefully wiping off all fingerprints. Again we adjourned.

We picnicked under some trees, thoroughly enjoying ourselves. Edie, it seemed, was now off the hook, unless Steinberg could prove that she had transported all the stuff up to Lompoc herself.

"Darlings," she said, "I feel like a new woman."

"Too bad you don't look like one," I replied.

"John, that has all the earmarks of an unkind remark, but, under the circumstances, I shall let it pass. There are more important things to discuss. How are we going to get our hands on Gotham? He seems to have vanished."

Well, the steel-trap mind of John Brett had some ideas about that, but it was, for the moment, keeping them to itself. I prefer, in cases such as this, to play my cards close to my chest. After killing off the gin and edibles, we packed the picnic stuff in with Steinberg and headed back to town. I wanted to stop at the post office to thank the nice lady for all her help.

The nice lady, having not yet positively identified her husband as being the nation's most wanted criminal, was still perusing the posters. She looked up when I came in.

"Find what you wanted?"

"Everything but Gotham himself. By the way, where does he hold the naked swimming parties?"

"What business is it of yours? You want to go to one?"

"Not really. Just curious."

"Go over to Jalama Beach. Them hippies are over there all the time, running around in just their skins, loving everybody. Disgusting."

"Isn't it. By the way, do you have Gotham's box registration card?"

"Course I do. Whaddya think, I don't keep my files up? Say, what are you, a postal inspector?"

"Good heavens, no," I said, denying such a repulsive charge as vehemently as possible.

"I guess not," she nodded. "Don't suppose they'd let any foreign trash have a job like that. Probably give away secrets to the Commies."

"Do you suppose I could see that card?"

She seemed to consider the proposition, running my request through the dark channels of her peasant mind. Finally, she agreed. "Don't suppose it'd do any harm, 'cept maybe to Gotham, and who cares about him, hunh?" Apparently, that was another thigh-slapper, as she dissolved once more into laughter.

When she recovered, she brought me the card. I suppose I should have had the foresight to equip myself with a Minox for such an occasion, but I'm afraid the thought never entered my head. A lot of thoughts never enter my head. In fact, there are those who claim no thoughts ever enter my head. Personally, I think they're wrong. On the other hand, I can't prove they're wrong. But it's much more comforting to think so.

At any rate, although I was minus Minox, I did not suffer from a dearth of deed. I whipped the document out of one of my Eisenhower pockets and quickly compared Gotham's signature with Gotham's signature. I mean the one on the registration with the one on the deed. They didn't match. Clearly, we had two Gothams. Clearly, things were not clear. I gave her back the registration card and started to walk out. As I left, she called after me.

"Hey, mister! Where'd you get the pink tenny-runners? Is that the latest thing in Hollywood?"

I deigned to ignore her.

"Hmph!" she snorted. "And *they* think *we're* weird!"

I drove back to civilization in silence, my mind puzzling out the intricacies of the case. By the time we got to Edie's, all was clear in my mind. Now all I had to do was prove it.

XVI

Steinberg recovered just as we got back to Edie's. First he moaned a little, then he stirred. Finally, with a heart-wrenching yowl, he pulled himself together.

"What happened?" were his first coherent words. They did not necessarily emanate from a coherent being.

"Would you like another martini?" Edie purred.

"Oh, God," Steinberg moaned. "I remember. I think."

We all went inside and spent an hour going over what we had found at Lompoc. The sum total seemed to be that we'd found some drugs and some Mud Dancers, in all probability, but not definitely, the same drugs and Mud Dancers that had been in the secret passage. Steinberg admitted that if (and he stressed the *if*) they were the same, Edie seemed to be at least partially off the hook. Her movements, he allowed, were closely enough documented over the past few days that she couldn't have ducked up to Lompoc and back again. I mentioned that she had been alone for a couple of those nights, but Steinberg mentioned that the house had been watched every night since the murders, and Edie hadn't left.

Edie was sufficiently buoyed up that she invited us all to dinner, which would have been nice except that Steinberg was hungover, and I wanted to get on with things. We exited.

I dropped Steinberg off at HQ and made arrangements to pay him a call the following morning. He agreed, provided I wear long pants and something other than the pink tennis shoes. I thought that was a bit narrow-minded of him, but what the hell, you can't have everything, can you? I took myself home and mixed a light drink. Then I began putting all the pieces of the puzzle down on paper, so when I talked to Herbie the next morning I wouldn't be my usual incoherent self. Once it was all laid out it made considerable sense, if I do say so myself. It was ugly, but it held together. Proving it, though, was going to take some help from Steinberg. Somehow, I thought I might meet with some reluctance on his part.

I appeared bright and early the next morning, nattily turned out in a conservative tweed jacket and heather pants, every inch the young English gentleman. Even Steinberg was impressed.

"I wouldn't have believed it," he said. "You almost look normal."

"So do you. The martinis must have helped the nettles. Your face, if you don't mind my saying so, is almost down to normal. The nose has a few days to go yet."

"The nose," he replied a bit testily, "won't go down without surgery. What's on your mind?"

"I thought we might go over the case," I said.

"Did you, now? You on the force these days?"

That set me back, but only momentarily. "I seem to be doing better than you," I pointed out.

"Not necessarily. Without you butting in, I could have hung Edith Wilson. Now I don't know what to think."

"But Edie didn't do it."

"It wouldn't be the first time we've convicted the wrong person," he said, folding his hands complacently on his tummy. "A conviction is a conviction. Support your local police."

"Are you quite finished?"

He nodded.

"Then tell me your theory."

"I already did. Simple. Mrs. Wilson called you with a phony story. Wilson had sold the Mud Dancer to Gotham, so she knew where it was. You bit, and went up and swiped the icon. She sent Harry out on another errand, to pick something else up from you. It could have been anything."

"At four o'clock in the morning?"

"Four o'clock, five o'clock. Who carres? Mrs. Wilson is a persuasive woman. Then she follows her husband, waits till you've given him the statue, then shoots him. As soon as you leave, she picks up the statue and heads for a phone booth on Olympic Boulevard that she's checked out before. You call her, and the call is relayed by the machine to the phone booth. She tells you to come over immediately, and you leave. But she ahead of you, and since Olympic is much faster than Wilshire, she gets to her house before you do."

"And the gun?"

"She dumped it in a lot."

"And then someone else found it, and took it and shot Calvin, then threw it back in the lot? A bit of a coincidence, don't you think?"

Steinberg agreed. "All right, you've shot my case full of holes. What's your theory?"

"Well, it isn't easy," I said for openers.

"With you, Brett, nothing is ever easy. But go ahead."

"All right. What have we got? A gun, a car, some drugs, two houses, an apartment, two bodies, God knows how many Mud Dancers and an odd lot of people. All we have to do is fit them together."

"Elementary, my dear Watson." His sarcasm was not appreciated, but I chose to overlook it.

"Everywhere we look, we find Gotham. He was involved in both houses and the apartment, he had the Mud Dancer twice that we know of and he seems to have been known to practically everybody. But he's elusive. Also, he doesn't exist."

"He what?"

"No such person. I have a copy of his signature on an old deed to the Wilson's house, and I saw his signature on the post office box registration card in Lompoc. You'll probably have to subpoena that card, or whatever it is you do. Anyway, the two signatures weren't even close. Even granted the thirty years' difference in their execution. So I don't think there is any Gotham. Instead, I think we have two people posing as Gotham."

"Any ideas about who they might be?"

"The latest one is easy. Hans von Berlin. When I looked around at the funeral the first time, von Berlin was there, but Gotham wasn't. The next time, Gotham was there, but von Berlin wasn't. I know what happened after we got into the nettle bush, but I'll bet von Berlin had reappeared."

"But how'd he do it?"

"At the funeral, all he would have needed was a mask and a wig. I was fifty feet away from him. Any other time, when he wanted to appear as Gotham, a good makeup job would do the trick beautifully. And I don't think he was Gotham much of the time. Don't forget, he lives in my building, but he's practically never there. And I'll bet he's practically never in Lompoc, either. Most of the time, Hans von Berlin is just Hans von Berlin."

"But you said there were two Gothams."

"Right. Von Berlin isn't old enough to have owned the Wilsons' house. So if Harry Gotham used to own it, there must have been another Harry Gotham."

"And I suppose you have that figured out, too?"

"Naturally," I said, trying not to sound smug. "Something has been going on in that house with drugs. They've been moving them in and out in Mud Dancers. And I think, since Harry Gotham's been around for years and doesn't even exist, that the drug operation has been going on for years. So we have to hook up an older man."

"Like Harry Wilson?"

"Why not? After all, Edie herself says he used to be a bootlegger. If he'd deal in illegal booze, why not illegal drugs?"

"Why not, indeed?"

"On the other hand, why would Harry Wilson foreclose on Harry Gotham's house if he already owned it?"

"Cover-up. Things like that confuse issues nicely."

"True," I agreed, "but there's something else. Wilson was just starting to get rich when he foreclosed on that house. He couldn't have afforded it earlier, and besides, he was still in Chicago. So Harry Wilson wasn't the first Harry Gotham."

"So who was?"

"What about the Mud Dancers? Who do we know that dealt in Mud Dancers besides the Wilsons and Gotham? James Hinman. And he's the right age to have been the first Harry Gotham. He's been an art dealer for years, and he could have been simultaneously dealing in drugs. The twenties were a good time for art dealers, but the Depression wasn't. So he must have been losing money on his legitimate operation. If he'd come up with a lot of cash to pay his mortgage, someone would have wanted to know where he got it. Someone like the Internal Revenue Service. So he let the house go. But I'll bet James Hinman has rather a large sum of money stashed away in Swiss banks and tied up in foreign real estate. Art dealers get around a lot."

"But why the change in identity?"

"Hinman got too old. The drug market is a youth market. So you have to have someone young to get around and make contacts and drum up business. Someone like Hans von Berlin, who could meet people his own age, then sell to them as Harry Gotham. Doesn't have to worry about getting caught, because Hans von Berlin doesn't deal in drugs. Just meets a lot of people. When he meets a junkie, Harry Gotham turns up later with the merchandise. Not many vice cops are actually junkies."

"True, true," Steinberg muttered. "Pity, isn't it?"

"Now, let me show you how it all worked. Hinman, as Harry Gotham, set it up years ago, and it was a one-man operation. He probably bought the stuff in France and brought it in stashed in his art works. Picture frames, hollow statues, anything. Then he stashed it in his secret passage and distributed it. Large quantities in Mud Dancers, small quantities any way possible. But then he lost the house. But why relocate? Why not just get an accomplice inside the house?"

"Like Harry Wilson, who deals in bootleg, anyway?"

"Like Harry Wilson. So the two of them run the thing together, Hinman for the money, Wilson for fun. But then the two of them started getting older. Hinman started having difficulties making contacts. So he brings Hans von Berlin in and sets him up with the apartment and the house in Lompoc to work out of. Von Berlin keeps his two lives separated very well. At his business, and most other places, he's Hans von Berlin. At the apartment and the house in Lompoc, he's Harry Gotham. Everything perks along nicely. Until trouble starts."

"And who's the trouble?"

"Calvin Kellerman Gunman, also known as Troy. Hans von Berlin began getting his lives a bit muddled. Got hooked on a junkie. Suddenly, there's a possibility that the peculiar relationship between von Berlin and Gotham might come to light. After all, if Calvin-Troy got picked up, there's no telling what he might say. Cold-turkey cures, I'm told, cause loose mouths. Among other things. Hinman and Wilson become aware of the problem, and good old Harry starts thinking things over. The structure's getting shaky, and besides, smuggling isn't as easy as it used to be. Too much new technology and too much pressure from people like you."

"We try," Steinberg put in. "God knows we try."

I ignored him. "So old Harry tries to pull out. After all, it just wouldn't do for a respected businessman to be caught in a drug ring, would it? Price fixing or tax evasion or unfair competition is one thing. But drugs? Not done. Simply not done. So he tries to get out. He announces that henceforth there will be no drug traffic through his house. Needless to say, this upsets Hinman's little applecart. One doesn't let a thing like he's got going just go down the drain. So Wilson has to go. Also Calvin, who may or may not have, but probably has, figured out the relationship between Gotham and von Berlin. After all, he's living in Gotham's apartment, and von Berlin can't keep his makeup on all the time. Besides, Calvin was still a little young for the dirty-old-man thing. Although you never know. Drugs make strange bedfellows. Well, be that as it may, that's what happened."

Steinberg leaned back and lit a cigarette. I could see him going over all of it in his mind, twisting it this way and that, looking at it from every angle. Finally, he spoke. "Brett, you amaze me. I owe you an apology. You may not be as dumb as you act."

"Thank you," I said, reeking of humility.

"Any ideas about how you're going to prove all this?"

Well, actually, I didn't. I'd been more or less counting on Herbie for some creative thinking in that department. Not, of course, that he'd shown much potential for creative thinking thus far, but it seemed to me that as one of Beverly Hills's finest, he had to have *something* going for him. "Isn't that your department?" I inquired innocently.

"Mmmph," he said, noncommittally. Then something seemed to occur to him. "What about the real Mud Dancer?"

"Just a souvenir. Hinman came across it, who knows where, and Wilson thought it would be nice to have it. Then he got worried about displaying it. I mean, how would he explain to Edie if another one showed up? After all, the house was crawling with them. So he had Edie put it in the garage. Then, occasionally, he'd pull one out, and Edie always thought whichever one happened to be out was the real one. Figured Harry had changed his mind and gotten it out of the garage. Actually, that was old Harry's biggest mistake, buying that real Mud Dancer and letting Edie see it. Once he stowed it, he figured he'd better display it now and then, just to keep Edie from getting worried and pulling the original out. But he kept wavering, probably, and then Hinman set him up for the kill. Had von Berlin, as Gotham, swipe the thing right under Edie's nose. She, being protective about her things, raised a stink. But Harry, knowing the thing was a fake and full of drugs, wasn't about to call the police. Edie insisted, and Harry refused. Finally, a compromise was reached. Edie had Gotham's address and knew from talking to him that he had a caseful of icons. So she called me and, unbeknownst to herself, set up poor old Harry. All Hinman's crowd had to do was wait for Harry to try to recover the icon and then plug him. You have to admit, they pulled it off."

"So they did," Steinberg mused. "So they did."

For a long time silence prevailed, and I assumed Steinberg was thinking. In all probability, it was a false assumption, but then, you never know, do you? At any rate, eventually he picked up his phone and gave some orders.

"Brett," he said when he was done, "let's got talk to a few people and see if we can get this thing nailed down. Then we'll go arrest our killer. I assume you'd like to be there?"

"Why, yes," I said. "I think that would be appropriate. After all, I did all the work."

Herbie gave me one of his sour looks, and we were off. I do hope Herbie will stop giving me sour looks some day. They're very disturbing.

XVII

Steinberg stopped at the front desk to pick up an envelope and then led me to a police car.

"Don't want to take the Sunbeam?"

"This looks more official. Puts the fear of the law into the criminal elements."

"If you say so . . . ," I agreed reluctantly, as I have repressed, deep in my subconscious, ugly memories of police cars. They are, I regret to say, connected with the problems I encountered on the native soil. I steeled myself, however, and joined Steinberg in the chopped down Black Maria. With a sense of direction of which I am still in admiration, he drove to Hans von Berlin's salon. We were greeted at the door by the charming receptionist, Elsa.

"You got tax cart?" she demanded. "Got to haff tax cart to come in here."

Steinberg flashed his badge. "Steinberg," he announced. "Beverly Hills police."

Elsa paled, and her teeth started chattering. "It vasn't my fault," she squalled. "I vas only acting under orders. Ve vere all in the party then. But I didn't believe. Not me. Down mit Der *Führer*."

Steinberg looked at me.

I shrugged. "I suppose von Berlin thought she'd go well with the Germanic decor," I said.

"Sit down, lady," Steinberg told her. "We aren't after you."

Elsa plumped into a chair, still murmuring about how she had only been following orders. Eventually, after we promised not to deport her to Israel, she settled down.

"Where's von Berlin?" Steinberg asked.

"Lunch. Out to lunch. Von't be back for haff hour." She paused and searched our faces. "You really not from the Nuremberg trials?"

"They've been over for twenty-five years, ma'am," Herbie tried to reassure her.

"For us it is never over," she moaned. "All ve vere trying to do vas save the world. But they never let us alone."

We left her muttering at her desk and went into von Berlin's office. I began poking around, and Herbie began taking fingerprints.

"They match," he said finally.

"What?"

"The prints. The prints all over this office, which I assume are von Berlin's, match the prints all over Gotham's apartment, which I assume are Gotham's."

"We knew that," I said a bit smugly.

"But we had to prove it, remember?" He had me there. I granted him a point. About then, von Berlin came in.

"What, may I ask, are you doing in my private office?" He tried to look overbearing but didn't bring it off very well. It's hard to be overbearing when you're only five feet six and are wearing a blue velvet Edwardian suit. The effect is more Little Lord Fauntleroy than J. P. Morgan.

"You von Berlin?" Steinberg said in his most menacing tones.

"I am. And who are you?"

"Steinberg. Beverly Hills Police Department."

"Indeed?"

"Just want to ask you a few questions."

"Planning to redo the department? God knows, it needs it."

Steinberg sour-looked him, and he shut up.

"Where were you the night Harry Wilson was murdered?" Steinberg demanded, getting right down to it.

"What concern is that of yours?" von Berlin replied.

"I'll ask the questions, if you don't mind."

"Are you arresting me?"

Steinberg considered the question, and I could see his computerlike mind flashing through all recent and relevant Supreme Court decisions.

"Not yet," he decided. "But if you don't cooperate, I just might."

"He means it," I put in. "He's been saying the same thing to me for days now."

"Shut up, Brett." After thinking it over, I did.

Von Berlin decided it was in his own best interests to cooperate.

"Well, now, let me see," he mused. "The night Harry Wilson was murdered. I suppose I must have been at home. Probably alone, although you can never tell, can you?"

"How well do you know Harry Gotham?" Steinberg said, appearing to change the subject.

"Gotham? Oh, I don't know. How do you mean that? I mean, what's knowing someone well?"

"OK. Let's put it on a scale. Do you know him A: very well; B: quite well; C: casually; D: nodding acquaintance; E: only by sight?"

"I suppose casually would describe it. We know each other professionally. I put him onto a job now and then."

That, I thought, was the understatement of the year. Steinberg almost flinched.

"Know him socially? Have dinner together? That sort of thing?"

"Oh, no. Lunch perhaps, once or twice. That's all. We don't travel in the same circles."

"Oh? What's he like? What kind of circles does he move in?"

"Why, I don't know, really. I only know we aren't in the same circles, because I never see him outside of business hours."

"Isn't he sociable?" Steinberg said, pushing the matter.

"Not really. Very cool, actually. Hard to know. I asked him to dinner once or twice, but he never accepted."

"Ever return the invitation?"

"Never."

"Hmm. That's strange. I thought you decorator types tended to be chummy. Swapped notes over Sunday brunch, and all that."

"Oh, we do," von Berlin agreed. "But not Harry Gotham. He's a very cool one. I don't think I know anyone who's even been to his apartment."

Steinberg pounced. "He lives in an apartment?"

"I suppose so," von Berlin said, beginning to look just the slightest trace nervous. "Most everybody does now, don't they?"

Steinberg looked disappointed. "Yeah. I just thought you might have been there and could tell me something about the place."

"Sorry. Never been there in my life."

Steinberg nodded, then changed the subject again.

"Nice office you've got here. Clean. I like a clean office."

That got to von Berlin. He puffed up like a blue goose.

"Yes. I insist on cleanliness. The last thing Elsa does every night before she leaves is dust everything in here. Goes over it all with polish every day. That's why it shines so nice. Lemon wax, you know," he said, lowering his voice confidentially.

"Have to remember that. By the way, seen Gotham lately?"

Von Berlin turned wary. "Is he in trouble?"

"Could be. After all, there was a murder at his place. We don't seem to be able to find him."

Von Berlin nodded, as if remembering. "Oh, yes. They've been talking about it on the street. Troy, wasn't that his name? Worked at Kauffman's?"

"That's the one. And Gotham hasn't been seen since."

"Well, I certainly haven't seen him. Not for over a week. But I'll let you know if I do."

"You're sure he wasn't here this morning?" Steinberg pressed.

Steinberg was being overly generous, if you ask me. I mean, how many chances do you give a rat to wiggle out of a trap? But von Berlin didn't seem particularly interested in wiggling.

"Positive. He hasn't been here since before the murders."

"Then maybe you'll answer a question for me?"

"Certainly."

"If you've never been to Gotham's apartment, and Gotham hasn't been here for over a week, and this office is cleaned every day, how does it happen that the fingerprints in this office match the fingerprints in Gotham's apartment?"

The air positively left poor Hans. I mean, he sagged. The blood drained out of his face so completely that I checked the floor to be sure he hadn't sprung a leak.

"Fingerprints?" he said finally. Apparently, nothing else was registering on his brain at that point.

"Yes," said Steinberg. "Fingerprints. You know, those oily little smudges we use for making identifications."

"Messy little things, aren't they?" I put in.

"Shut up, Brett," Steinberg said.

I did.

Von Berlin continued his wilting act and finally settled into a pale green chair. Even in shock, his decorator's instincts had come to the fore. He had chosen to sink into a chair that was dyed to match his complexion. Also, the green went nicely with his blue suit.

"Perhaps," he suggested in a very tentative voice, "Gotham might have been here this morning after all. I could check with Elsa." He got up in preparation to leave.

"Sit down, von Berlin," Steinberg commanded.

One thing I'll say for Steinberg, when he commands, people obey. Von Berlin sat down again.

"I think," Steinberg continued, "that we'll have no trouble proving that you are Harry Gotham. I imagine you left a few prints at the place in Lompoc, too, didn't you?"

Von Berlin nodded. "What made you suspect?"

"The stunt at the funeral. That was bold. Very bold. But Brett here noticed that when you were there, Gotham wasn't and when Gotham was there, you weren't. Also, we found two Gotham signatures that didn't match."

"I didn't kill anyone," he said. But his tone didn't sound convinced.

"We'll see," Steinberg said. "Want to go with us while we have a little chat with James Hinman?"

Von Berlin sagged even further. "You're onto him, too?"

Steinberg allowed as how we were.

"But . . . but . . . I was only a messenger, really."

"Selling drugs is hardly acting as a messenger," Steinberg pointed out. "However, since you were really the little fish in the pond, I imagine things will go easily for you. Assuming, of course, that you're willing to testify against Hinman."

Von Berlin nodded dumbly.

"Too bad Wilson's dead," Steinberg mused. "I'd like to have gotten him, too. Operating a drug ring under my nose all these years." He shook his head as if he couldn't believe it could have happened. The three of us left. Poor Elsa, still sitting at her desk muttering about the Reich, didn't even bother to ask for our tax cards on the way out.

We arrived at Hinman's shop a few minutes later and brushed past his receptionist. Too bad, really, as she was quite an attractive girl. Would have liked to have chatted with her a while. Business, however, before pleasure. An old adage, if I'm not mistaken.

It didn't take long to break Hinman down. Without von Berlin, of course, it would have been impossible. Hinman would have done better to go ahead and bump off von Berlin, too. He certainly was the weakest link in the chain.

We trotted the two of them off to the slammer, both protesting their innocence of any murders. Their protestations, of course, had a hollow ring. The protestations of murderers always do.

Steinberg and I had one last call to make. I was sure Edie would be pleased to have him apologize personally for his accusations.

XVIII

"Brett," Steinberg said as we drove to the Wilsons', "this is going to be touchy."

"Call me John."

"It's still going to be touchy."

"Edie's a good sort. She'll forgive you."

"Still, what if she doesn't? Her bank holds the mortgage on my house."

"You should have thought of that before you jumped to those ridiculous conclusions about her." I'm afraid I sounded smug, but it seemed to me that I had good reasons for it.

We parked the car in front of Edie's house and knocked at the door. She answered it herself.

"Christ," she said, seeing the police car, "am I going to be dragged off in chains again?"

"I'm afraid I owe you an apology, Mrs. Wilson," Herbie said, groveling manfully. "May we come in?"

"Do. I think daiquiris go well with apologies, don't they? Marie!" she called.

Marie came down the stairs, absolutely radiant in a pants suit.

"New maid's uniform?" I asked.

"She doesn't wear a uniform anymore," Edie explained. "I promoted her to personal companion and secretary. It seems more fitting."

We all settled in the study, daiquiris in our hands.

"Now, tell all, and don't leave out a single grim detail," Edie said.

So we told them the story, leaving nothing out. I'm afraid Edie didn't like it about Harry being involved, but, on the other hand, Harry was dead, and she figured it was better to have a dead Harry involved in drugs than a live Edie involved in murder. Sound thinking, if you ask me.

As for Marie, her uncle's duplicity came as something of a shock. At first she refused to believe it, but when the whole thing was put together for her, there wasn't anything she could say. After it was all told, Edie had a question.

"But how did they set Harry up to bump him off? And which one of them did it?"

"Simple," said Steinberg. "Shall I explain?"

"Why don't I mix us another round of drinks first?" said Marie, rising.

"Don't, Miss Kellerman," Steinberg said. "If more drinks are to be made, I'm sure Mrs. Wilson will be happy to make them."

"But Marie makes better ones than I do," Edie protested.

"True," I said. "But God knows what she might put in them."

"What a horrible thing to say." Edie looked shocked.

"How about it, Marie?" I said.

"I don't know what you mean."

"Then I'll tell you. Edie, I'm afraid old Harry didn't count on something. He didn't count on James Hinman putting a spy in his house."

Marie got up again and moved toward the desk. But this time Steinberg had a gun in his hand when he told her to sit down.

"Don't you think two is enough, Miss Kellerman?"

Edie's mouth fell open, and for once in her life was speechless. Finally, she gurgled a little. "Marie? Marie shot Harry and that boy? But . . . but he was her brother!"

"She didn't know it at the time."

"But . . . but how?"

"It wasn't difficult. The night you called me, she simply followed Harry in your car and shot him. But she had a neat trick up her sleeve. She'd set your phone-relay machine to put all calls through to a phone booth on Olympic Boulevard. Probably did it that same night, having previously found a booth in the right location. Don't forget, Hinman had already decided to have Harry removed from the scene, so they had plenty of time for advance planning. Anyway, after she shot Harry and knew that I'd seen it, she was pretty sure that I'd call you. So she went to the phone booth and waited. As soon as I called you, the relay machine threw the call to the phone booth, and Marie picked up the phone there while you were talking to me from here. But the phone company's records make it look like you weren't here at all. According to them, the call was relayed to the phone booth, putting you there. That, coupled with the fact that it was your car I saw, and your gun that was used, put everything so far pretty much onto you.

"Then she drove back here, having left the Mud Dancer and the gun in a vacant lot where von Berlin, as Gotham, could pick them up later. She got back into the house through the secret passage, and you never even knew she'd been gone.

"Later that day, she went to Gotham's apartment to make sure von Berlin had taken care of Calvin. Don't forget, at that point she had no idea that Calvin was her brother. She thought his name was Troy, and she hadn't seen her brother for years, anyway. Von Berlin, though, had lost his nerve, and Calvin was still very much alive. So Marie, without thinking, picked up your gun and shot him herself. That was a mistake. If she'd called her uncle, he would have thought up something better. She realized it was a mistake and panicked a bit. That's when she dumped the gun in the vacant lot again. I suppose if you're told to shoot someone, then put the gun in a vacant lot, then every time you shoot someone, you'll put the gun in a vacant lot. Not very imaginative."

"But why did Gotham and Calvin drug you?"

"Oh, that's simple, really. Don't forget, I'd just shown interest in a Mud Dancer. It was probably filled with drugs. So they drugged me. They weren't particularly worried about it. Von Berlin knew he wasn't going to be doing the Gotham thing much longer, and he also knew Calvin was about through among the living. So they drugged me and dumped me back in my apartment.

"After Marie finished off Calvin, von Berlin told her I'd been up there, so she decided to come back later in the day as the ministering angel. Plays the part very well, if you ask me."

"Bastard," Marie snarled. "And I thought you were so dumb."

"Dumb but lovable," I said, remembering all her tender ministrations.

"What about the Mud Dancers that disappeared from the secret passage?" Edie wanted to know.

Personally, I'd been hoping she wouldn't ask that question. It was something that had been bothering me for quite some time, but I had sort of decided that if I didn't mention it, maybe nobody else would either. No such luck. Steinberg and Edie were looking at me. I began to squirm. The looking and squirming intensified.

"Well?" Steinberg said.

"Yes. Well. . ." I began.

"Oh, for heaven's sake." It was Marie. "I ought to let you try to wiggle, but I might as well tell you. They never disappeared. They're still down there. Uncle James got the drugs out, but he didn't have time to get the Mud Dancers."

"But they were gone when we took Steinberg down there," I said.

"No, they weren't. They only appeared to be. I'll show you."

We all trooped once more into the secret breach, as it were. Marie opened the cabinet that had held the Mud Dancers, and it was still empty. Then she pushed a button under one of the shelves, and the whole shelf unit slid up and was replaced with a second unit. There were the Mud dancers, all in their neat little rows.

"Well, I'm damned," I said. "I never thought of that."

"About the only thing you didn't think of," Marie snarled. There wasn't much left of her ministering angel role.

We closed up the passage and returned to the study. Herbie called the police department for a car to come and get Marie, and we all had another drink. It seemed the least we could do for Marie. Sort of a farewell daiquiri. But we didn't let her mix it.

The fuzz came for Marie, and suddenly the three of us were alone.

Steinberg looked at his drink speculatively. "Wouldn't you know?" he muttered. "The damn maid did it."

"Who else would do it?" Edie wanted to know. "You certainly wouldn't think I did it, would you?"

Apparently, she had forgotten that he had. Oh, well, Edie was like that. Forgive and forget, was her motto. Literally.

"Well, anyway," she went on, "it's all over now. And I'm going to take you both to Chasen's for dinner. I'd have you here, but I'm afraid I'm having a slight servant problem. Is eight o'clock all right?"

When you're invited to Chasen's, any old hour is all right. Any old hour at all. Chasen's is like that.

XIX

I was back in the old French Château, which, as I have previously pointed out, is neither French nor a château. It does, however, have nice new copper plumbing, and I was enjoying myself in the shower, humming a few pertinent bars of "Hail Britannia." A resounding tune, "Hail Britannia."

I popped myself out of the shower and was busily drying myself off with the old school towel (a remnant of my lost youth) when the building began shaking. Sudden visions of a new murder flashed through my mind, and I waited for the phone to ring. It didn't. I was relieved. I mean, how much can one take?

I pulled the personal self together as best as possible, trying to find something to wear that would make look look as if I could not only eat at Chasen's but pick up the check as well. Of course, I didn't want to dress so well that they actually presented me with the check. That could lead to all kinds of embarrassment that I shall not go into here. Next time I write home to the native soil, I must try to get the hush money increased. Inflation, if I may be permitted to say so, is a terrible thing.

I packed myself into the Sunbeam and made my way to the appointed trough, arriving at the appointed time. A remarkable feat. Chasen's, apparently, has salutary effects on one, quite beyond their customary anointing of the taste buds. I found Steinberg cowering just inside the door.

"I say, Herbie," I greeted him. "Not bellying up to the old bar?"

He looked frightened. "What do they get for drinks here?" he whispered.

"Who knows?" I shrugged. "I have a system. I put them on the dinner check. That way I never know. What you don't know can't worry you."

The door burst open, and Edie charged in, resplendent in white.

"Out of mourning?" I asked.

"Proclaiming my innocence," she said. "I'm returning to my public life."

"How nice. But what about your fond memories of poor old Harry?"

"You mean Harry the Push?" she said, "I haven't forgotten him. I'm wearing black undies."

"Well, I suppose it's better than nothing," I said. Herbie settled for looking shocked. For a cop, Herbie looks shocked very well.

The maître d' tried to seat us at a rear table, but Edie insisted on sitting close to the door.

"I want to tell all my friends I didn't shoot my husband," she explained.

"Of course, madam," he said. "I quite understand."

I'm glad he did. It's comforting that headwaiters understand such things.

Edie got us all supplied with drinks, after cautioning Herbie about drinking too many martinis; then we settled down to business.

"All right, John, tell us. How did you know it was Marie?"

"Quite simple, really. I think I knew from the start. If it wasn't you, it had to be her."

"But how did you know it wasn't me?"

I drew myself up. I mean, what a terrible question. She shouldn't have had to be told.

"My friends," I said, "simply don't do such things."

Well, that set them on their ears. Herbie, particularly, was impressed.

"And on that, you decided that Marie had done it?"

"Oh, that and other things. I wasn't lacking for evidence.

"What evidence?"

"Well, for one thing, when Marie came in with breakfast that first morning, she looked worn. Tired out. Not at all like a girl who had had the traditional eight hours. I assumed that if she hadn't been sleeping, she must have been doing something else. Murder seemed as good as anything. I mean, she was a servant, after all, and the servant class . . . well, need I say more?"

Edie nodded sagely. She understood completely, of course. As for Herbie, I really didn't expect him to understand. He didn't. But he accepted.

"Then when we were at the morgue, viewing Calvin's rather unattractive remains, she said something. If I'm not mistaken the words were, 'Why do you suppose people always take on a younger look when they die?' Now, theoretically, Marie hadn't seen her brother for at least ten years, but she knew he looked younger in death. How could she have known that unless she'd seen him a lot more recently than she was claiming? So if she was lying about that, I assumed she must have been lying about a lot of other things, too."

"John," Edie said, after digesting it all, "I'm shocked. I simply don't understand you. I don't understand you at all."

"Oh? What don't you understand? Maybe I can elucidate." I like to use words like that now and then. Lends me a certain *panache* I don't otherwise have.

"How could you make love to her, knowing what she'd done? It seems . . . well, it seems immoral."

"Not at all," I said munching a crab leg. "Highly moral, really. I mean, I didn't intend to marry her, but, on the other hand, I didn't have to worry about violating her honor, either. It didn't seem to me that she had any honor left. Lots of sex appeal but no honor, if you know what I mean."

"Brett," Steinberg said, for once looking at me with admiration in his eyes, "you have a remarkable mind. Truly remarkable."

I went on munching my crab leg, but inside I felt proud. Very proud indeed.

THE END